For Brooke

'Hope'

is the thing with feathers

That perches in the soul

And sings the tune – without the words

And never stops – at all

– Emily Dickinson

Library of Congress Cataloging in Publication Data

THE PRINCESS & THE PARAKEET
Written by Marc Clark
Edited by Marian Grudko

Book and Cover design by Marc Clark and The Tim Coston®

ISBN-13: 978-0-9910345-2-9 (e-book)
ISBN-13: 978-0-9910345-8-1 (paperback)
ISBN-13: 978-0-9910345-7-4 (hardbound)

10 9 8 7 6 5 4 3 2

December 2018

First Edition: April 2017 (hardbound)

Library of Congress Control Number: 2018965994

For more fun by Marc Clark, visit www.TheFablesKingdom.com

❀ ❀ ❀ ❀ ❀ ❀ ❀

The Princess
&
The Parakeet

❀ ❀ ❀ ❀ ❀ ❀ ❀

by

Marc Clark

Blah Blah Blah

PRESS

LOS ANGELES - FT. MYERS

CONTENTS

~ *I* ~

The Princess

If Princess Brooke had only been born once like the rest of us, she wouldn't have believed so completely in miracles. But being born twice? That was proof positive: anything was possible.

Anything.

That's what she was thinking as she skipped up another flight of stairs.

The fact that she was ever born was a miracle – her parents told her time and time again (as I'm sure some of yours have). Her understanding of that gave her a power that rivaled the wisest minds. To her, every hour was precious; every minute, a new blessing; every second, a jewel to dazzle her.

She wasn't sappy about it either. She'd never say, "Life is like a beautiful flower, you must drink from its nectar," or anything like that. More likely, you'd find her chasing the servant's children through the hallways, pretending to be an ogre, making them giggle and scream, or spending hours in the nursery, lying in a sea of pillows with a bright-eyed baby making up tales of Penelope, The Perfect Princess, who was positive purple peonies made you sneeze. With each puff of a 'P' the infant would smile from the breeze on its face, and an, "A-a-a-a-a-chooooooo," would send them into peals of laughter.

Princess Brooke would dress in the brightest colors on her darkest days and stroll through the castle corridors, singing.

Ask her for a favor, she'd deliver it tenfold.

Pay her a compliment; she'd stick it in her pocket.

Take her hand; she'd offer her heart.

I can say for certain, your life would have been better for knowing her. There's beauty in the world if you look for it; there's faith, hope, and love - she possessed them all: doling them out freely to anyone who crossed her path, with a charm that wouldn't fail. The word "Grace" is seldom used anymore, maybe because she was the last person to embody it so completely.

Moving through the wide, sunlit halls of the castle, you'd be hard-pressed to pinpoint exactly what it was that told you she was royalty, yet there was no denying it. You'd also never know she was under a curse and had been even before she was born (though she'd insist it was only a spell).

It took every ounce of her princess-restraining-training not to run up the last flight of stairs to the top floor of the main castle, where her present would be waiting.

Waiting. Three years. Doing without other presents didn't bother her, but the waiting for this one ...

The King and Queen extended their hands to Brooke as she reached the landing.

Her mother kissed her cheek, "Happy birthday, darling."

"Really happy," the Princess said.

Her father gave her shoulders a squeeze and kissed her on the head. "Happy birthday, Princess. What's it like being a twelve-year-old?"

"Umm ..." Brooke said, but they were facing the door to her new room now, and all of her attention was there.

Queen Jessica pushed it open.

The scent of fresh flowers was the first thing that hit the Princess, and it made her smile. The room was filled with her favorites: tulips, roses, hibiscus, and buttercups. Running her hand along the bed to the fine, sturdy footboard, she shook her head in disbelief, "It looks like a room I've lived in for years. How did you do that?"

The place was bright and sunny, warm and comfy, richly crafted. It was the tall ceiling that set the room apart. Builders had replaced the old one with a grid of wooden beams, creating a checkerboard of four-by-four foot sections.

Footsteps echoed from the roof above.

"It's happening right now?" Brooke said, unable to keep her hands from shaking.

Her father nodded.

"Where? Which one?" she said, following the sound of the worker's footsteps on the roof to the middle of the room where they stopped. She pointed to the square panel at the center of the grid.

The King and Queen nodded as they joined her.

Brooke was trying to catch her breath. "I didn't think we'd be doing this first thing," she said.

The sudden pounding of hammers made her jump.

The wood creaked, a crack of sunlight, metal bars, and thick workman's hands gripping the edge of the square. One big grunt, and the center section came out.

A cool breeze swept in through the open skylight.

The family stood just beyond the square of sunlight on the floor.

The King said, "Whenever you're ready."

Brooke shook her head. Each parent gripped her hand, bringing back the stillness in her. Their touch always did.

"Okay," Brooke said, sucking in the electrified air. This was it. She'd plotted, planned, worked for so long for this moment. Everyone had. "Here we go …"

She let go of their hands. Took one step into the sunlight. No change. Good.

It was always that second one, though.

She took another step. Standing directly under the skylight …

… the Princess disappeared.

A moment later, Brooke reappeared alongside her parents.

It hadn't worked.

She didn't need to put on a brave face for them. It'd been a long shot. She knew it. Each failure took her a step closer to success. She searched the room as if the answer might be out there somewhere.

The sound of the workers on the roof brought her back.

Right, it's not over yet.

The workmen lowered a thick pane of glass into the empty square. Secured it, and then gave the King the okay.

Brooke didn't hesitate this time. She simply walked to the center of the square, calmly turned to face her parents, and shrugged. Of course the glass pane worked. What was the big deal?

Her face erupted into a smile, and she spread out her arms, welcoming the warmth of the sun on her face.

After a royal family group hug, they headed down to the great hall and Brooke's birthday celebration began.

Throughout the day, she'd drag guests up the stairs to show off her beautiful room. On each visit, more glass panels had been installed.

After saying farewell to the last of the revelers, she plodded up the stairs holding her mother's hand.

"Oh," Brooke said, as soon as she stepped into her room. With all of the glass panels in place and the night filled with stars, it was like standing on top of the world; she was about to say so to her mother when something drew her attention. The glass in the center of the roof was missing. Directly below it was a large planter holding a young sapling with bluebonnets, dandelions, and pink primroses sprinkled around its base.

"I thought it'd be nice to get a little fresh air in the warmer months," the Queen said, "and you can never have too many flowers."

"I can't," Brooke said.

"It's an apple tree," Queen Jessica said, helping her remove her dress.

Brooke gasped. She closed her eyes, reciting, "There was an orchard once, within the castle walls ..."

The Queen smiled, helping Brooke into her nightgown. The Princess climbed into bed while Queen Jessica arranged the covers and sat next to her. "Are you sad, Mother? That we couldn't break the spell?"

The Queen gave her girl a squeeze. "We bent it pretty well."

"Mmm," Brooke said, snuggling in. "Tell me again, 'There was an orchard once ...'" she said, watching the leaves of the apple tree, waving, silver in the moonlight.

"There was an orchard once, within the castle walls ..." her mother began ...

❀ ❀ ❀ ❀ ❀ ❀ ❀

... It's no longer there, nor is the innocence of my youth.

It was a bright, sunshiny day, and I was dancing around the rows of twisted trunks, singing a made-up, silly song when I heard a noise coming from the sky. I looked up through the tangled branches to see a boy, sitting high up, his features shadowed by the sun.

"It's forbidden to climb these trees," I told him.

"Really?" he said, as he plucked an apple and took a bite.

"Nor should you be eating the fruit, especially the chosen ones from the top."

"Hmm," he said, looking off. He then dug his teeth into the apple, held it in his mouth, and without a thought, jumped all the way to the ground.

It should've startled me, but I was so fascinated by this bold creature, I forgot to be afraid.

His hair was blond and tousled, and his green eyes sparkled with mischief. His clothing was ill-fitting and oddly matched. There were patches of clean skin here and there, but in most places, the dirt had dug in so deep, it had become a part of him.

I'd never seen a street urchin up close before, and I doubt he'd met any Princesses – after all, he could be imprisoned just for speaking to me. We faced off like wild animals, meeting for the first time, unsure if the other was friend or foe.

"Do you always do what you're told, Princess?" he asked.

❀ ❀ ❀ ❀ ❀ ❀ ❀

Brooke jumped in saying, "Well, yes, of course. Why would I do otherwise?

"Hey," the Queen said. "Who's telling this story?"

"Did you really say that?" Brooke asked her, doing an impression of her mother, "'Why would I do otherwise?'"

"Something very like it," the Queen explained. Brooke was still looking at her sideways. "Darling, if you want facts, read a textbook. This is a memory. Two very different things."

"Oh, I see," Brooke said. "You made it up."

Her mother looked at her open-mouthed.

Brooke smiled. "Just checking. Go ahead. 'So, you've never eaten forbidden fruit?'"

The Queen shook her head.

"He probably never said that either," Brooke added under her breath.

❀ ❀ ❀ ❀ ❀ ❀ ❀

"So, you've never eaten forbidden fruit?" he said, tossing the half-eaten apple aside. "Never climbed a tree, like this one? Up to the high branches, where you can see over the castle wall?"

I shook my head.

"You mean to tell me you never sat in this orchard, staring at that branch, the one that goes over the wall," he said, pointing it out, "and saw yourself crawling across and jumping down on the other side? Never wanted to run off to the city streets where there's danger around every corner, or out to the country with nothing but grass and hills – no walls to hold you in?"

I stared at him, open-mouthed – how he could have known about a dream I'd never shared? How could he know how desperately I wanted to escape all the rules and responsibilities, and run free?

"Well, you can dream it, Princess ..." he said, hopping onto a low branch, "... or you can live it," he finished. I felt myself stepping closer to him, as though in a trance. "But not in that dress," he said, laughing.

The nerve.

He scurried up the tree, yelling, "See ya' tomorrow." Then he swung onto the branch, tightrope-walked it over the wall, and with a wave goodbye, dropped out of site. Gone.

❀ ❀ ❀ ❀ ❀ ❀ ❀

"And you didn't sleep a wink that night," Brooke said, helping her.

"That's right."

"Because your heart was racing," Brooke added, "and your imagination was out-running it, with all the adventure you two could have beyond the castle walls."

"Am I going to tell this story or are you?"

"I like that part," the Princess said before settling back into her mother's arms, trying as hard as she could not to yawn, but yawning anyway.

"I don't encourage this kind of behavior, mind you," Queen Jessica said.

"Oh, I know," Brooke said. "It's terrible. Scandalous."

The Queen nodded and smiled.

❀ ❀ ❀ ❀ ❀ ❀ ❀

The next morning, before dawn, I tiptoed down the cold stone stairs to the handmaidens' room. Shaking with fear, I snuck into the maid's quarters and borrowed the clothes of a girl I knew to be my size, then hurried back to bed before Nanny came to wake me.

Morning lessons were a blur. The moment they finished, I rushed through the kitchens, out the back, put on the servant's garb, and waited for the adventure with my apple thief to begin.

For hours, I sat and stood and paced. I forced myself to look away, believing, sure as surety can be, that he'd be there when I looked back. He never was. A guard found me by torchlight, huddled at the trunk of the tree. Your grandfather carried me back to my room, too worried to punish me. I returned day after day. I made excuses for him at first: he'd been captured climbing the wall, thrown into prison and was, even now, digging his way toward me. I practiced my, "How dare you treat me like this ..." speech a hundred different ways.

On my third day of coming up with the cruelest tortures imaginable (little-girl-cruel, with no blood, and I'm wearing this pretty blue dress ...), I'd finally had enough. I climbed that stupid tree, cursing it as though it had stood me up for two weeks, scooted across the stupid branch, over the stupid wall, hung by my hands for a moment and dropped to the stupid ground.

The foul odors and clanging commotion of the city streets hit me at once, and my anger turned to panic. I backed up against the wall. 'How could I have not heard this in the orchard, or at least smelled it – ugh?'

I searched for the branch to take me home. Why did I come? What was I thinking?"

Then I heard, "Over here," and turned to see the boy, sitting against the wall a few feet away, whittling a small stick. He wasn't wearing his misfit outfit anymore. No. He looked surprisingly dapper in his tattered clothes. He knew it, too: winking at me as he hopped to his feet. He strolled toward me, as though he'd done absolutely nothing wrong.

I was about to give him the verbal lashing I'd committed to memory when he said, "That's what you're wearing? Really?" And one side of his mouth curled into a crooked smile.

"Alright." Then he took off into the dusty street, dodging the oncoming horses and carts.

He stopped, right in the middle of the road, and yelled back, "What are you waiting for!" Motioning with his head for me to follow, he said, "Come on."

I thought, "He'll be run down by the oncoming traffic – so could I, if I follow him." But follow him I did.

❀ ❀ ❀ ❀ ❀ ❀ ❀

The Queen stopped, feeling the slow, steady, breathing of Brooke against her chest.

She rested her cheek in the curls atop the slumbering Princess' head. "What a cruel legacy I've left you with, my darling," she whispered. "And I'm afraid the worst is yet to come."

Queen Jessica watched the sapling leaves flutter in the wind, and held her little girl tight, beneath a ceiling of stars.

~ *II* ~

The Parakeet

J t was late the next morning when Brooke finally opened her clear green eyes, sat up in bed, stretched and yawned - still a little drowsy. The chamber was flooded with sunlight, and it brought a smile to her face. She pulled her knees up under her chin, admiring her lovely apple tree. The blossoms surrounding ... wait, something was moving ... bending a branch near the top.

Oh. It was a little bird. Beautiful: a snow-white Parakeet with golden feathers on its head.

Brooke watched the bird hop from branch to branch. Something about it ...

Her delicate brows came together to form a frown. What was it? She couldn't put her finger on it, as though the image had unlocked a door, way in the back corner closet of her mind, up on a shelf she couldn't quite reach.

In an instant, the wrinkles vanished. The little bird stirred something very clear, very deep in her heart. It reminded Brooke of the spell put upon her (not a curse).

"My father could have been a Parakeet, just like you," she said to the little bird.

The Parakeet floated down to the lip of the giant planter and cocked its head from side to side in Brooke's direction. "You don't say," he said. "How is that possible?"

The Princess shot up and gasped. "You ... you can talk!"

The Parakeet gasped, too. "You ... you can understand me!"

"Why, yes I can," she said, jumping up and scooting to the edge of the bed. "This is so exciting!"

"Isn't it tweet? I mean, neat?" the bird asked.

"It's both," she said. "It's the most amazing thing."

"I've been in this feathered form for years, and you're the first person who's been able to understand what I'm saying. You have no idea what a relief it is," he said, with a little chirp.

"I'm sure I don't," she said. "But a huge one, I bet."

"It's as though a dark cloud has passed; as if a weight has been lifted from my ... I feel like I could ..." then he took off into the air, "... like I could fly," he said, laughing, and soaring around the room.

"And you can," Brooke said, clapping her hands.

The bird swooped in and around the furniture and over Brooke's head, "My heavens," he said, making another circle, "this is a spectacular room. I don't believe there's anything quite like it in the world."

"Oh, I suppose that's true," she said, taking in the room,

"You'd know better than me about the world. I know that I'm very lucky to have it."

The Parakeet landed on the bed's footboard to get a better view of the Princess.

"And I'm very lucky you found your way here so I could share it with you. I'm an especially lucky person," she told him. "Hey, how did you find your way here?" Her eyes lit up. "Did you hear stories about me? Do they tell stories of Princess Brooke in the taverns and inns? Oh, oh, did someone send you? Are you on a quest?"

"No, no one sent me," he said, "I ... I'm sorry, should I know you? Are you famous?"

"Hmm," she said, "You know, I don't really know. I hadn't thought of it until just that moment. It's possible, though. It would explain a lot, wouldn't it?"

"Explain what?" he asked.

"You. Me. This," she said, spreading out her arms.

"I'm afraid I'm at a loss ..." he said, stretching out his wings. "I was merely attracted by the sun's reflection off the glass, and when I saw the opening–"

"No, that's not it," she said to herself, waving off the idea with her hand, thinking. The Princess took a new look at the white bird. "Tell me, are you charmed?"

"I do believe I can be somewhat charming," he told her, puffing out his little chest.

"You certainly can be, and you are," she assured him, "but what I meant was: are you under a spell of some sort?"

"I am, yes. How did you know?"

"Well, there's the whole talking bird thing, for one," she said.

"Ahh. Good point."

"And then, it just so happens that I'm under a spell, as well," she said, watching for his reaction. (She couldn't really tell. Parakeets don't have facial expressions, so it can be difficult figuring out exactly what they're thinking sometimes.) "I thought, perhaps ..." she said, drawing it out, "... we might be kindred spirits." Her face lit up. "Doesn't that sound fascinating? 'Kindred Spirits?'"

"Interesting," the bird said, nodding its tiny head.

"Was it a sorcerer?" she asked. "That changed you?"

"Why, yes, it was," he answered. "Were you cursed by a sorcerer as well?"

"Not cursed, no, but put under a spell by one, yes," she said. "And quite by accident."

"You don't say?" he said.

"I do, too, say," the Princess said back. "Oh, do you want to see?" She hopped out of bed without waiting for his answer.

"I'm not sure ..." he said, watching her run to the middle of the room in her nightgown and stocking feet. "Please don't harm yourself on my account."

"No, it doesn't hurt," she yelled back.

She stopped just short of the skylight and put her hands on her hips, looking at the planter taking up most of the space under the opening. She tried pushing the planter. "Could you give me ..." she said, catching herself. She turned back and smiled at the bird. "Never mind."

The Parakeet flew over to join her and fluttered around the tree, trying to make sense of what was going on. He watched her as she tried moving the huge planter using her arms, then her back – pushing off with her feet. Then she stopped. She didn't quit, just stopped. She walked around it, looking for ... something – he couldn't tell what. Then she turned around and did the same thing with the room. Searching.

The Parakeet followed her gaze, trying to figure what she might be looking for.

"Yes," Brooke said, as a smile took over her face, and the room came alive. She dashed off.

The Parakeet followed. His wings began fluttering like a hummingbird. He zoomed from one side of the Princess to the other. She grabbed a low-back chair near the tea table, weighed it and shook it in her hands, nodding to the bird who for some reason, nodded back, giving his approval. This chair would be good enough, sturdy enough – for what, he had no idea, but he was in on it now.

The pair hurried back to the center of the room. The Parakeet zipped around the tree to make sure ... Well, he didn't really know why. It seemed like the thing to do, so he did it.

Brooke shoved the back of the wooden chair up against the planter, making sure it was secure. Again, she nodded to the bird. Again, he nodded his approval. It was good. Sturdy. Ready. For whatever it was that was going to happen.

He zigzag-followed Brooke to her bed. In two seconds, her

nightgown was over her head – off, into the air. He should've been shocked: a girl in undergarments. No time for that.

One sock off. Then the other.

Brooke faced the tree, dug her feet in, and revved up. Breathing fast. Grinning wide. "I've never done anything like this," she told him.

He nodded. He understood nothing. No matter.

"Here goes," she said and took off toward the tree.

The bird kept pace.

Running at the tree. A chair in front. What for? Almost there. Will she jump over? Foot on the chair. She was going to …

He was flying so fast he missed her second foot touching the edge of the planter.

He swung around. It's not … She isn't … She wasn't there. He circled … She didn't hit the tree. Nothing moved.

Then he heard a giggle. He whipped around and there she was, a few feet back from the planter.

"What is it? Did you not jump?" he asked.

She nodded.

"You didn't? How did you–"

"No, I mean, yes, I did jump."

Everything had happened so fast. The excitement of it all. He flew toward the Princess and then back to the tree, then repeated it. "I'm sorry, I don't …" He couldn't even finish. He wasn't sure what it was he didn't know. He should go. The skylight. Go.

"No, no, I'm the one who should be sorry," Brooke said, moving toward him. "Here," she said, offering her fingers for him to perch on. "We'll take it slowly."

The Parakeet fluttered back and forth a little more. He could go. No. No. Alright. He took a moment, and then slowly glided over to the young Princess, landing softly on her forefinger.

"There," she said. "Better?"

He took a breath. "Better," he said.

"I got a little excited, I guess," she said.

"As did I," he said.

"Let's see," she said and started doing that thing she does, looking around the room. Saying to herself, "A perch ... It's such a nice word: perch." Then, "Well, this'll have to do."

The Princess gently lowered her hand, allowing the Parakeet to step off onto the back of a large sofa facing the fireplace. "Remind me. I have to have perches made for you, everywhere."

"Yes, alright," he said, as she rushed off.

She took a position a few feet back from the open skylight and turned to the bird. "Nice and slowly," she said, then did a little curtsy, as though she was about to begin a performance. "Just watch." Keeping her eyes on the bird, she took a step. Then another. One more. Then onto the chair against the planter. Then with her eyes widening, she stepped up onto the planter ... but she didn't.

He could've sworn ... The Parakeet looked back to where the Princess had begun her little show, and there she was, waving at him.

Brooke rushed over to him and knelt down to be at his eye level. "Do you see? I can't go outside. I can never go outside."

Quoting, *"You shall never leave, come what may, remain inside for every day."*

"Never?" the bird asked.

She shook her head.

"Not ever?"

"Yesterday," she said, closing her eyes and spreading her arms, "was the first time I felt the sun on my skin – through glass." She lay back on the floor. "Last night I slept under the stars."

"All by accident you say?" the Parakeet asked.

"Yes, I do say," she said, sitting up, smiling. "I have quite a bit to say if you'd care to hear it," she added, holding up her finger.

"Oh, very much, Your Highness," he said, flittering over to her finger. "Though my ears are impossible to find, I can assure you I'm an excellent listener."

"Well," she began, "... there was an orchard once, within the castle walls, where my mother spent much of her life as a child ..." Then she went on to tell the beginning of the tale of how she came under the spell; much the same way as it was told to her.

When Brooke reached the place in the story where her mother ran into the street to join the apple thief, she stopped, just as the Queen did the night before.

"Oh ..." she said, closing her eyes and putting her hands to her heart. "She had no idea where she was going or what was going to happen. Everything she'd ever learned being a Princess was no good to her at all. Ah ... Isn't that just ...?" Then she sighed.

"Yes, it is," the bird said.

"Okay, I'm going to skip ahead here – just for now," she said.

"What?" he said, ruffling his feathers.

"I'm definitely going to tell you," she explained, "... imagine: every minute they spent together was filled with danger. She had to sneak away, and he could be put to death if they were caught. This went on for years and years. But I was telling you about the spell, so ..."

"Right," the bird said, hanging its head. "I understand. Sticking to the point. Yes. I remember." He looked off. "I read a lot of books – too many, one might say – have said, actually."

"Me, too," Brooke said, "... and same here."

"Really?" the Parakeet said, cocking its head toward the Princess. (Again, it was hard to tell what he was thinking, but if I had to guess, I'd say that he was both surprised and pleased.) "In the middle of a book, have you ever felt as though you're not reading any longer? As though you've become a part of the story?"

"Oh, yes."

"When that occurs, I'm happy to follow these people wherever they go – grateful even, when a character veers away from the plot. I don't know ... It's as if I've been given a glimpse of them off the page, sharing something private. It's ... somehow, more personal."

The Princess stared at the little bird, not saying a word.

The Parakeet adjusted its wings. "It's silly, I know," he said quietly.

She shook her head. Then turned away from him.

He heard her sniffle a couple of times, and then wipe her eyes.

When she turned back, she was all smiles. "I'm really glad we left a hole in the ceiling," she said.

"As am I, Princess."

"'As am I,'" she repeated. "I love the way you talk."

"Why, thank you," the bird said.

"You speak so well," she added, "way better than your everyday Parakeet."

The bird gave a little bow.

"Obviously, well educated."

He nodded.

She waited for more, but when he said nothing, she continued, "So ...?"

"So ..." he repeated.

"Oh, my goodness," she said, shaking her fists. "Won't you please just tell me who you are? Are you a knight? A nobleman. No, a Prince. Are you a Prince?"

"Why, do I come off as Princely? Is it how I carry myself?" he asked, showing off his fluffy chest again.

"Oh, definitely. Everything about you just screams, 'Royalty'," she said. "Plus, I figured, why would a sorcerer put a spell on an ordinary person?"

"Good point," he said. "I was christened, Prince Benjamin Mordecai Higginbotham, but you can call me Ben if you like."

"Hmm. Ben. Ben," she said, trying it out. "Ben, would you pass me the peas, please? Tell me the truth, Ben; does this dress make me look fat? Ben, you're such a scoundrel." Then she laughed. "Yes, I would like to call you Ben. I would like that very much."

"Without lips, it's difficult to tell," he told her, "but right now, I'm smiling."

"Oh, I can tell, alright," she said, and then added, "I'm Brooke."

"Your Highness," he said with a bow.

She looked at his little birdy face, noticing how smoothly the feathers lay, one on top of another, how surprisingly natural the bright golden feathers were. "I hope ..." she said, "... well, a lot. I mean, I hope for a lot of things, or about a lot of things. But that, you'll ..." She sat up and started over. "Your Highness, I would like to offer you the hospitality of the palace. We would be honored to have you as our guest ... if you want."

Ben looked this way and that, not saying a word.

"If you're not too busy ... or anything," she added.

"Umm ..." he began, "I would be most grateful to accept your ... Yes. Of course, yes."

"Oh, good. Goodness!" Brooke said, "I'm glad that's over. Why was that so hard?"

"I don't know," he said. "It was a bit uncomfortable."

Brooke suddenly noticed how she was dressed. "Aaa. I'm not fully dressed," she said and jumped up. "Why didn't you tell me?"

"I wasn't ... I hadn't ..."

She leaned toward him. "I'm teasing," she said.

"Frankly, I'm just trying to keep up," he told her.

"Okay. It's this way," she said, heading toward her dressing room.

"Yes," the little bird said.

Brooke stopped and turned around. He hadn't moved.

"What is it, Ben?" She walked back and knelt down to be at his eye level. "Did I say something wrong?"

He shook his tiny head, 'No'. After a moment, he said, "It's only ... there are so many wonderful gifts wrapped up in the package that is you, my new friend. I am, without a doubt, the luckiest Prince in the world to have found you."

Now, Parakeets don't have tear ducts, so I can't honestly say that Ben shed a happy tear at that moment, but I know a Princess who'd swear he did.

"I like it so much when you call me friend," she told him, lightly scratching his breast with her fingertip. She leaned in and gave him a tender kiss on the head. "So, you're lucky, too, huh?" she asked.

He nodded.

"You know what they say about luck?" she said, getting to her feet.

"Who are 'they'?" he asked, taking flight.

"You're silly," she said as they walked and fluttered across the room. "Okay. 'Some people' say that there's no such thing as luck; it's just being able to see all the wonderful possibilities around you and grabbing one." She put her finger up, stopping Ben in mid-flight.

He looked around and realized that he'd followed her into her dressing room, "Oh, sorry," he said, quickly zipping back out.

Brooke pulled the door behind her, leaving it open just a crack so they could talk.

"Others – not 'they'– say that luck is when what you've learned meets the chance to use it. But you know what I say ..." she said, peeking out the door, "... luck, is contagious. It's a disease, and you caught it from me." Then she ducked back in.

"I have so much to learn from you," he said, landing on the tea table.

"Oh, I'm sure you know way more than I do," she yelled back.

"I beg to differ ..."

Brooke's laughter came from the closet. "You 'beg to differ'?"

"Alright then," he said – if it were possible for him to roll his eyes, he would have. "I don't agree with you. You see, I am merely intelligent, whereas you, as it turns out, are smart."

"Okay, I'll buy that," she agreed, re-entering the room in a bright blue dress.

Ben had never seen the Princess fully dressed. He watched her as she pulled the ribbon from her hair, releasing streams of curls that fell about her shoulders. Her mouth was moving, but he couldn't quite make out what the words were. His wings brought him up into the air, floating behind her as she crossed the room. Then she did the strangest thing; she leaned forward and began brushing her hair, upside down. What was she doing? When she stood upright again, he understood completely. Every highlight the sun had to offer got caught up in the swirling ringlets as they bounced into place, framing the delicate features and flushed cheeks. He'd never seen anything like it.

She put her hands on her hips and looked at him sideways. Oh, no. Did she ask him something?

"Yes?" he said, hoping that would cover it.

"Now," she said, "may I interest you in a guided tour, Prince Benjamin ... Medicine ... Higgly-wiggly?"

"Close enough," he said. "I would be delighted, Your Highness. Lead the way."

~ *III* ~

The Orchard

Brooke pushed open the doors to a small, unassuming room with an entire wall of windows made of cut glass. The afternoon sun shining through the upper panes sprinkled the room with little diamond-like reflections. "This is my mother's sitting room," Brooke said.

"It's charming," Ben said, hovering in the doorway.

"Come on in," Brooke said, motioning with her head. "She usually has tea here. You'll meet her then. She loves that I visit this room."

Ben took off, exploring.

Princess Brooke closed the doors and took a seat in the bay windows in the middle of the wall of glass. Ben joined her, looking out at the colorful patchwork of flowers, trees, shrubs, and hedges that made up the royal gardens.

"Yes, this room should definitely be shared," Ben said, as he set down next to his friend.

"Do you know what this entire garden used to be?" she asked him.

The Parakeet looked up at her and shook his head, "No, what?" When she didn't answer right away, he looked at her more closely.

It hit him, suddenly, with a gasp of air. Brooke nodded slightly, seeing that he figured it out.

They both returned their attention to the garden beyond the windows.

This time, the Parakeet repeated the words: "There was an orchard once, within the castle walls ..."

"I must tell you about that first day, at least," she said.

❀ ❀ ❀ ❀ ❀ ❀ ❀

That first day, my mother ran into the crowded streets after her apple thief. Dodging the carts and horses, she got turned around. It was so loud she didn't hear the man yelling. She was about to be trampled when a hand reached through the crowd, grabbed her wrist, and pulled her to safety.

"Try to keep up, Princess," the boy told her.

Before she could catch her breath, he was pulling her down a side street, then another. Pulling her – a Princess. She didn't dare free herself from his grip – what would happen to her in this place?

The truth is, she didn't want to. It was so terribly exciting.

Everything was happening so fast; everyone was moving, and the noise – she could scarcely make out what the boy was saying, pointing out shop windows, warning about dark alleys, avoiding one rough character or another, but she did learn that his name was Beauregard, but most people called him, Beau.

❀ ❀ ❀ ❀ ❀ ❀ ❀

Brooke watched her friend as she mentioned the boy's name.

"What?" Ben asked.

"Was that the name of your sorcerer?"

"Oh. I can't be sure," the bird explained, "Everyone simply referred to him as the Sorcerer. He didn't speak to many people."

"Darn," she said and went back to the story.

❀ ❀ ❀ ❀ ❀ ❀ ❀

Before long, the noise and movement of the city streets began to fade; avenues became wider, buildings became shorter, grass grew up between them, then gardens and hills with cows and sheep grazing.

My mother found herself smiling, uncontrollably. She looked over to the young man who'd brought her to this place.

Beau had let go of her wrist long before – now he was offering his hand, and she took it. He walked her to the top of a hill, and they both fell backward onto the thick grass under an old oak tree. She lay there, staring up at the wide open, blue sky for what seemed like hours: the old oak, stretching its limbs, the rich earth beneath her, breathing in the country air, filling her lungs with a peace she'd never known. Her thoughts and cares floated away like the distant clouds, and she was free.

It frightened her that she'd so easily broken any rule she had to, to gain her freedom. She looked over at Beau, this stranger who seemed to know her better than she knew herself. He smiled back at her with that crooked smile. As if he knew, scared or not, she would break those rules again and again.

That she was never meant to be – nor would she be again – a good little girl.

❀ ❀ ❀ ❀ ❀ ❀ ❀

Ben whistled. It wasn't a tweet or a twitter, but a real whistle.

"I know. Shocking, right?" Brooke said. "Here's what I think happened. You know how they say rules are made to be broken?"

"They?"

"Oh my gosh. People. People say."

"I never heard people referred to as 'they,' is all," Ben said. "I understand now. Yes, I have heard people express that."

"Alright," Brooke said, looking at him sideways. "I think she figured out that breaking a rule doesn't make you a bad person," she explained. "If that's true, then shouldn't you question every rule?"

"Ah, yes," Ben said. "Rule one: Obey every rule without question. Rule number two: Know which rules to break."

Brooke smiled.

"Or ... so they say," Ben added.

"Look at you," Brooke said, pushing her friend lightly with a finger.

If he could, I'm sure Ben would've smiled back.

"My mom and Beau became the best of friends. He showed her how to survive on the streets, and she taught him to read and how to walk and talk like a gentleman. As you may have guessed, their friendship turned into love. "

"My father says, 'Being young is imagining you're on a pirate ship on the open sea – when actually you're in a bathtub watched over by your parents. Being young and in love ... a rock has more sense and probably listens better, too.'"

❀ ❀ ❀ ❀ ❀ ❀ ❀

My mother was coming of age to be married.

Beau had become an apprentice to a strange physician who lived out in the woods. He told her the old man was a sorcerer, but Beau had a habit of fiddling with facts to make a story more exciting.

I don't know what it's like to have your heart broken, but I pray I never have to feel the pain she felt when her father sat her down one winter's day and told her she was to be married to a Prince from across the seas. She cried and cried until there wasn't enough salt left in her body to season another tear.

Then she had to tell her beloved, Beauregard.

❀ ❀ ❀ ❀ ❀ ❀ ❀

"It was there," Brooke said, pointing out the window. "See that stone bench?"

Ben nodded his little birdy head.

"It used to have an arbor covering it," she told him. "Nothing but empty vines tangled around it on that winter's day – the stone, cold beneath them."

❀ ❀ ❀ ❀ ❀ ❀ ❀

Watching Beau's face as she repeated her father's terrible news was almost more than my mother could bear; that crooked smile became a thin, hard line; the light in his eyes went out, and the blood drained away. He clutched his heart as if she'd driven a blade through it. "No ..." he told her, "you love me. You said you loved me."

"I do."

"You can't take that back," he told her.

"I'm not."

"Alright, alright. It'll be okay," he said, more to calm himself. "We just have to figure it out ... We'll have to run away. We have to," he said, taking her hand. "I can't give you the kind of life you're used to."

"None of that matters," she told him, "You know that. But ..."

"What?" he asked, searching her face for an answer.

"I ... I can't do this," she said and collapsed into his arms.

"We can do anything. Remember? As long as we have each other," he said, holding her, running his fingers through her hair.

"No," she said, mostly to herself. They wouldn't have each other. She would be alone, even at her wedding to a stranger. "We can't," she said, not able to look at him. "We can't run away. There's nowhere in the world a Princess can hide. When they find us, they'll put you to death."

"I don't care about me. We have to try."

"No," she said, feeling empty already. "I used to think I was strong – you made me feel invincible." She shook her head at the thought. Living without him was already too painful. His death? "I could never bear that ... I couldn't."

"We can't give up. There has to be something we can do," he

said, pulling her up to look into her face. He started to smile, but something stopped him. He let go of her and backed away.

He saw what Princess Jessica had already accepted: in spite of all their efforts, the rules and obligations had won after all.

He rose with anger building inside him. He'd never given up on anything. He began yelling at her, calling her a coward. Seeing the streams of tears flowing down her cheeks – he railed at the unfair world, the people in it, the system, money, anything or anyone until the fight left him, and he fell to his knees.

❀ ❀ ❀ ❀ ❀ ❀ ❀

"That was the last she saw of her first great love and her only friend. In that very spot," Brooke said, before growing quiet.

Ben looked up at the Princess, staring out the window. He inched closer and pushed his tiny head beneath the palm of her hand.

She turned to him and smiled, softly petting his smooth golden feathers with her thumb. "I've heard the story so many times, I feel as if I've lived it," she said. "Does that make sense?"

Ben nodded.

"These windows weren't here back then," she told him. "Mother had them put in. They said their goodbyes in secret, just as their whole lives together had been." She leaned in closer. "When I said it was the last she saw of her him, it doesn't mean he didn't show up again. Twice, actually, but he was no longer the young man she'd fallen in love with."

"No?" he asked.

"No," Brooke told him, shaking her head slowly. "He'd

changed ... and not at all, for the better."

❀ ❀ ❀ ❀ ❀ ❀ ❀

The first came the day before my mother was to marry my father. A white dove landed on her windowsill: in its beak, a note on gold parchment. She knew it was from him the moment the bird cocked its head to one side. She felt her heart beating again. "Had it stopped on that cold day?" Beau hadn't been lying about his apprenticeship with a sorcerer. As she took hold of the note, the bird vanished in a cloud of white smoke.

He asked to meet her in the orchard – their orchard – this place.

She could barely breathe, running through the castle and out to the rows of trees, now hanging with ripened fruit.

She spotted him right where she knew he'd be; at the end of a row, leaning against a tree that had one branch reaching over the castle wall.

She stopped suddenly. Something was wrong. Something bad. His eyes and hair had turned black. He was so thin, and his skin was sickly and pale.

As she stepped closer, she noticed the fruit on the tree had rotted, much of it fallen to the ground around him.

"I've seen you with him," he said in a dark voice she couldn't recognize.

"What's happened ...?" she asked.

"I've seen you playing for him, singing, dancing with him ... laughing," he said, nodding his head. "I see it now. You love him."

"What? No. How could you say that?"

Lashing out, he cried, "Liar. I've seen you!"

"You know that's not true. You know me."

"I will turn your fiancé into a toad," he said.

"You mustn't, that's horrible," she said. "Can you really do that?"

"Or a disgusting rodent."

"Stop it. Stop it right now," she told him. "You can turn him into a Parakeet if you want. It won't make any difference. It's not about him. There'll always be another prince or lord for me to marry."

❀ ❀ ❀ ❀ ❀ ❀ ❀

"Oh, my word," Ben said.

"Yes, a Parakeet," she agreed. "Just as I said. It's the same man, isn't it? Your Sorcerer and mine?"

"It may very well be," Ben said. "It would explain a lot."

"Okay, okay ..." she said, shaking.

❀ ❀ ❀ ❀ ❀ ❀ ❀

"No," Beau said, pointing his finger at her face. "I saw you. It's him you love now. You're like the fruit in this rotten orchard; reaching for the sun, turning your rosy cheek to capture his warmth. But you'll wither on the branch because there is no love in you."

"How can say that?" my mother cried. "Why are you doing this to me? Please stop."

"Oh, I will," he said with a laugh, "I will." Then he gave her that crooked smile, but coming from his thin, gray face, it made her shiver, "I'll find a way to stop you from destroying another heart; to repay you for what you've done to me."

His eyes welled up, and his head started shaking. He looked as if he might break and crumble to the ground.

She reached out a hand toward him. He was in so much pain.

He took hold of the trunk of the tree with both hands, trying to hold himself together. "You ... you let me believe ... you let me hope ..."

He looked at the branches and grew angrier as if they were the cause of his agony. He shook the trunk with all his might. The tree, the roots, the ground beneath them shook: rancid fruit falling around them.

Mother ran for the castle.

Beau kept shaking and shaking: more and more of the trees – the entire orchard – quaking. Fruit festering. Raining down. Smashing, thick in her hair. Staining her clothes. Squishing underfoot. Screaming. Crying. She ran. Not looking back. She ran till she reached the safety of the castle door.

❀ ❀ ❀ ❀ ❀ ❀ ❀

Her mother's voice joined in as she said, "Till she reached the safety of the castle door."

Ben and Brooke turned to see Queen Jessica standing in the doorway.

Brooke smiled at her, and together they said, "Once inside, I looked back and saw that every tree, every one, had lost its fruit. The leaves, the trunks and branches were on fire, flames reaching to the sky."

At the mention of fire, Ben's feathers ruffled, and he started flapping his wings. "Fire. You didn't say there was fire."

Ben fluttered around in different directions. Everyone was talking at once:

"What is it? What's wrong?" Brooke asked him.

"I need some air," Ben gasped.

Queen Jessica, coming closer, "Darling, where'd that bird come from?"

Ben started flying his body into pane after pane of glass, and again, they spoke all at once:

Ben cried out, "Don't any of these windows open?"

"It's okay, Ben," Brooke said, getting up.

Queen Jessica looked around. "Who's Ben?"

Ben screamed, "Can't breathe. I need air."

Brooke unlatched a window while everyone still talked over each other:

Brooke pushed the window open, "Here, here," as Queen Jessica urged, "Darling, be careful."

Ben yelled, "I can't breathe. Where is it?"

"Ben, here," Brooke called out.

Ben was darting back and forth, "I have to get out," while the Queen tried to get Brooke's attention. "What is going on?"

The Parakeet found the window Brooke opened for him and flapped his wings as hard as he could.

Brooke yelled out the window after him. "It'll be okay, Ben."

He'd already flown so high, he was merely a speck in the sky.

"Don't go," Brooke yelled.

Queen Jessica joined her daughter at the window. "What was that?" she asked. "Who were you talking to? What was wrong with that little bird?"

"What if he doesn't come back?" Brooke asked. Tears welled up in her eyes. "He has to come back. He just has to," she said, wrapping her arms around her mother's waist.

"Who, darling?" she asked her little girl. "Did someone give you a bird for your birthday?"

"He's not a bird, Mother," she said, looking up at her with tears streaming down her cheeks. "He's a Parakeet." Brooke buried her head in the folds of the Queen's dress, sobbing.

"A Parakeet," Queen Jessica repeated in a whisper, holding her little girl.

The Queen searched the blue skies for the little bird.

~ *IV* ~

The Fever

The King peered into the dim light of the sitting room... he opened the doors, letting in the light from the hallway.

There she was. Where she spent most of her days, and where she'd go when she snuck out of bed at night: on the cushions of the bay windows, one of them open, so her friend could find his way in.

She'd fallen asleep, leaning against the glass, shivering.

"It's freezing in here," he said, reaching to shut the window.

"No, please," she begged him, "leave it open."

"Alright," he said, lifting her into his arms. "Up we go."

The Princess moaned and half-opened her eyes to see her father's face. "He's coming back," she said, struggling to get out of his arms, "I have to wait for him."

He held her in place, firm, but soothing. "Of course he's coming back. Maybe not tonight, though," the King reassured her. "You're kind of warm." He put his cheek against his daughter's forehead and frowned.

Worried servants were waiting for them outside the door. The King motioned for Brooke's nursemaid to come close and whispered to her. She hurried down the hall.

The King carried his daughter upstairs, saying, "You know Parakeets are wanderers and not usually night flyers."

"Not Ben. He's different."

"Mmm," he said, nodding.

"What makes you think he'll come back to your mother's room?"

"I just know."

"Alright," he said. "You should always go with what you know. Only fools are ruled by the opinions of others."

"And obedient daughters," she added.

"Well, if you know of one, point her out to me," he said. "I'd like to see this rare creature."

Brooke wrapped her arms around her daddy's neck, nestling in. Rocked by the gentle movement of his steps, she let her eyes close.

He slid his little girl into bed, pulled up the comforter, and sat on the edge facing her. Her cheeks were flushed.

He looked up and nodded as the nursemaid showed the physician in. The doctor was still wiping the sleep from his eyes, having been roused from his bed.

The King placed his large hand on the forehead of his little Princess, and she opened her eyes, "What if he went back to face the Sorcerer?"

"From what you tell me, he's pretty smart."

"Yes, but he's just a little bird," she said, yawning.

"Go to sleep, Princess," he said in his soothing voice. The one fathers use to let you know that everything will be all right. "He'll find his way back to you."

"What if he's in danger?" she asked, barely awake.

"Go to sleep," he said again, softer, stroking her hair.

And she was asleep.

❀ ❀ ❀ ❀ ❀ ❀ ❀

Just like that, she was awake, and she was flying.

It took her a moment to know what was happening. She'd never had a dream where she flew. She'd never dreamt so vividly of being outside, of being free. Oh my. It was all so beautiful. It didn't seem like a dream at all. No, it couldn't be. She felt her shoulders straining and the jolt forward with each flap of her wings.

This is what the air tastes like up here: thinner, but clean.

She looked down, and, oh my. Oh, my goodness.

It was too high. Breathing – she couldn't breathe.

Did she forget to flap?

She was falling. Oh, no. "I can't. I can't."

❀ ❀ ❀ ❀ ❀ ❀ ❀

Back in her room, the physician stepped away as Brooke kicked her feet and pounded her fists into the bed. "I can't. I can't." The Princess was covered in perspiration.

The King calmly ran his hands down the length of Brooke's arms. "Of course you can, Princess," he said in that deep voice.

"Anything's possible." He kept repeating the movement and the words. "Of course you can. Anything's possible."

❀ ❀ ❀ ❀ ❀ ❀ ❀

"Of course you can," Brooke, the bird, said to herself. "Anything's possible." She closed her birdy eyes and spread her wings ... and soared. Banking to the right, opening her eyes and swooping left.

She got back into her rhythm: one, two, three flaps – push, push, push, and soar. Now she could look at the earth below.

She was following a road of dirt and stone. A wide path cut through rocky terrain, dotted with leafless trees and evergreens. Up ahead, it looked as though the road ended. Running into a ... what?

Suddenly a shiver of fear overtook her, taking over her whole body. What was it?

❀ ❀ ❀ ❀ ❀ ❀ ❀

Queen Jessica entered Brooke's room as the King and nursemaid pulled the bedcovers over a teeth-chattering Brooke.

The Queen was followed by two servant girls: one, she told to gather some dry clothes. Nightgowns. The other set a kettle down on the tea table.

Queen Jessica began preparing tea, telling the other servant, "Send one of the boys from the kitchen to fetch a pail of well water – the coldest, and keep it coming."

"How's our little girl?" the Queen asked, turning to the King. His face told her all she needed to know ... but didn't want to hear.

❀ ❀ ❀ ❀ ❀ ❀ ❀

The road she'd been flying above looked like it ended at a wall of some kind. All along its base, some sort of uneven, white fence.

Brooke, the bird, could see now that it wasn't a wall but a forest: thick, dark, and moving. She could also see why she was so afraid.

The white fence consisted of piles of skeletons from beasts she couldn't recognize, bleached white by the sun.

The forest was alive. Not naturally, like leaves blowing, or boughs bending. It was unnaturally rotting and growing at the same time, constantly. Trees taller than they should be, trunks and branches, knobby and bony like disfigured, arthritic hands. Plants grew out of the undulating mass of rot on the forest floor, opening spindly leaves and bringing forth grotesque puss-oozing flowers. Slithering, clutching ivy twisted around the plants, strangled them, and then moved on to another victim.

Pumping her wings up toward the sky, she reached the roof of the evil forest. It, too, was in a constant state of growth, movement, and death.

Just ahead, she saw what looked like of mix of giant rat and monkey, skittering across the prickly-spire tops of the trees.

Directly in front of her, a massive open mouth, riddled with rows of razor-sharp teeth shot out of the forest, clamping down on the rat-monkey, ripping it in two. The mouth snapped again quickly, gobbling up the bloody remains of the monkey-rat.

❀ ❀ ❀ ❀ ❀ ❀ ❀

"No, no," Brooke yelled out, trying to crawl out of bed.

The King wrapped his arms around her as she flailed around.

She wore herself out struggling to get free, finally collapsing back into the sheets.

The nursemaid handed Jessica a fresh, cool cloth as she joined her family on the bed, gently wiping the soaked strands of hair from her baby's face. "What is it, darling? Where are you? Come home to us, baby."

The Princess blinked her eyes open. She seemed to recognize her mother's face. She reached out a limp, weak hand toward her. The Queen grasped it in both of hers and kissed it. "Come home, Brooke. Come home to us."

Brooke nodded, ever so slightly. The beginning of a smile pulled at the edges of her lips.

Queen Jessica nodded back and returned the smile, placing her cheek on her girl's little hand. She kept nodding her head. Brooke followed her bobbing head, and the movement rocked her to sleep.

The King laid her back down, and the women went to work, removing the damp clothing and linen, bathing her quickly with cool cloths and getting a fresh, warm nightgown on her, placing her back down on fresh linen, warm and clean.

When the Princess was tucked in and sleeping soundly, the Queen went over and poured some tea.

The King watched her, looking a bit confused. "Shouldn't she sleep?" he asked.

"It's for us," she told him, pouring the second cup. She brought him one and sat down herself. "This is just the beginning," she told him before taking a sip.

The King closed his eyes for a moment and then took a sip of the strong brew.

The parents turned to their little Princess, listened to her slow and steady breathing, and steeled themselves for the coming days.

❀ ❀ ❀ ❀ ❀ ❀ ❀

Far above the evil forest, as high as Brooke-bird could go ...

Parakeets aren't made for great heights or long journeys; their little bodies are built for short distances and sharp turns to avoid predators in a tangled jungle.

Parakeets don't have a sense of smell either, but whatever gasses the forest emitted were thick and palpable. Her sharp eyes clouded over, and her wings grew wet and heavy; a sour, moldy-metal taste coated her tongue, but it was the never-ending death-cries of other-worldly creatures coming from below that struck fear into her little birdy heart.

She tried to get back into her rhythm: one, two, three flaps – push, push, push, and ... Oh, no. Each time she tried to soar, she'd drop a little closer to the forest. She couldn't climb higher. It took all of her power to keep flapping – the second she stopped, she'd fall closer to the nightmare below.

Closer. Her eyes would sting a little more, her wings grow

heavier; the sick would rise in her throat.

Closer. Any further down and –

Snap. The orange beak of a huge black bird-creature slammed shut, bursting through the jungle top. Screeching. The giant beak opened again, slobbering, stretching, inches from her tail-feathers.

Brooke zipped right then left, another snap of teeth behind her.

No escape. No choice. Brooke-bird pulled up short, and then shot straight down, into the dark, into the monster's den.

She felt the rush of air behind her – the black bird chomping down, barely missing.

Deeper into the jungle she went – the air thick and dripping wet, snapping branches on her tail – the black bird in pursuit.

Her wings were getting heavy. She cut one way, then back, feeling the black bird pulling closer.

Everything around her was a growing horror show of mangled trees and mutilated beasts zipping by. Her ears, full of screams and cries of the jungle coming alive, cheering for blood. Hers.

On one side, a serpent spread wings and dove at her. On the other, a fifty-pound cockroach whipped out its green tongue. She dove toward the moving earth, layer after layer of prickly vines whipping tentacles at her from every direction.

Weaving in and out. The black bird closing in – cut right. Drooling teeth snapping shut – cut left. Turning sideways, slipping between branches.

The big bird crashed through.

Up ahead, a flower, as big as a horse, spun around to face her, its petals whipping furiously in hungry anticipation.

The black bird gained on her.

The flower spread out. Its stamen unfurled, dozens of knife-sharp thorns at the ends.

Brooke-bird pushed forward, straight for it. The black bird screeched, stretching out its slavering craw.

The flower opened its huge stigma-mouth, rows of red teeth, roaring, salivating.

Just as the thorns surrounded her, she dropped, straight down, cutting two feathers on the way.

She ducked into the folds of the flower's giant petals, listening to the wild screeching death cry, the gnashing of bones and beak as the flower devoured the black bird.

No beast would brave the hungry flower to come for her.

As darkness fell, the flower folded up its petals, creating a warm cocoon as she slept.

~ $\mathcal{V}$ ~

The Sorcerer

She was sleeping again, finally.

It was the second day of her fever.

The King felt her little hand relax and let go of his. Brooke had been clutching, squeezing, and digging her fingers into the skin of his hand for the last hour.

The King covered his eyes with his other hand, squeezing his temple. Each breath he took helped straighten his arched back and rounded shoulders. When his hand fell away, he was sitting tall as a King, leaving the tortured father behind ... for now.

The physician and the women swooped in with fresh linen, a new nightgown, cool water, and sponges.

The Queen slid her arm around her husband's, hugging the tensed muscles. Closing her eyes, she rubbed her cheek against his shoulder, and then giving it a quick kiss, she joined the women.

"There's my sleepy Princess," she said quietly. "Let's get you all clean and comfy."

❀ ❀ ❀ ❀ ❀ ❀ ❀

The setting sun took on a reddish glow as she peered through the gaseous mist above the forest.

Her arm-shoulder-wings were beyond sore, beyond tired. She could only count: one, two, three flaps – push, push, push, and bank left for a few brief seconds of rest. Then again: push, push, push, and bank right. Not knowing how much longer she could keep it up.

She'd been at it all day. Once again, the sun was sinking behind the hills. It wouldn't matter soon. The winged monsters below would be right at home in the dark.

Demons are made for the night.

She could hear the sound of rustling, waking beasts growing louder as each minute passed. She had to reach her destination within the hour. Less. But what was it? Where was she going? What was she after? Push, push, push, bank left. Push, push, push, bank right.

Up ahead, stars began to dot the sky. It wouldn't be long now. Push, push, push, bank left. One star hung very low in the sky. It was brighter than most. Push, push, push, bank right.

Wait. Not a star ...

Right in front of her, a huge beast shot up to the sky. She darted hard right to miss it, and a black shadow with the wingspan beyond that of an eagle's passed over her.

Push, push, push, bank left. The light ahead was growing brighter.

More shadows taking flight: to the left, right, all around.

Push, push, push, right. She could make out what it was now. A castle. A tower. No, too tall for a tower.

Push, push, push, left. Giant mosquitos with glowing blue eyes lifted off from treetops by the hundreds.

She had to flap harder – dodging this way and that – to avoid them.

It was a tower. Taller than any she'd seen, and yet, familiar. Flap, push right. A wall surrounding it. Yes. Flap, push left. Both higher than she could hope to fly. Push right. Almost there. Almost.

No. Coming at her. The sharp needle, glowing eyes, of a giant mosquito.

This was it.

The evil bug pushed forward aiming its needle right for her.

Push hard right. Hard left. She hit the bug's body with her beak.

A scream. Blinded: puss and blood soaking her.

Shaking hard. It split in two. Parts falling. Shadows swooped in, fighting over the remains.

Then quiet. Cool air. Clean air.

She'd made it. The evil forest was behind her.

Push, push, push, and soar.

Just soar. Just for a while.

❀ ❀ ❀ ❀ ❀ ❀ ❀

"She's fighting it," the Queen said, wringing a cloth over the pail, dabbing one flush cheek, and then the other, laying it across Brooke's forehead.

The physician finished his examination and placed her limp arm back under the covers. Every wrinkle of his face carried the burden of worried parents and two sleepless nights. "We'll know soon," he said, being sure to meet the eyes of both his Queen and King. "The fever has to break."

Before the Queen could ask the question, he answered, "It must."

❀ ❀ ❀ ❀ ❀ ❀ ❀

"Who built this wall?"

She was slowing down, wings aching, and still not to the top.

Push, push, push, push, push … There. Ah. Finally. She dug her talons into the stone, unsteady. Her little heart beating. Her little breast, heaving.

Looking down, she had to tighten her toes. It was dizzying. She felt weak. Birds don't perspire, but she felt as if she was.

She turned around and looked up, and up, and up. The light of the tower was too high. She'd never make it.

Taking flight, she felt better. Circling the tower, soaring. Maybe there was an entrance, and she could make the trip in stages – a few floors at a time? Nope. Nothing.

A gust of wind caught her wings, lifting her higher. "Oh, that's nice." When it passed, she looked up. No, the light was still far above.

Then she got an idea.

Parakeets see the world slightly more enhanced than humans, more colorfully. Warmth is tinted with oranges and reds. The cold takes on bluer hues. She flew out from the tower, searching the moonlit skies. There it was. Through her birdy eyes, she saw what looked like a river of orange coursing through the deep blue night: warm air, rising. She made a beeline for it, flew alongside, and then swerved into the stream.

She floated in the airstream with no effort at all, moving faster and faster. "How did I know this?" she asked. Before she could answer, the stream lifted her higher. Up ahead, it bent to the left, swinging her away from the tower. She veered right instead and shot straight up toward the light.

There was a wide, stone balcony protruding, and the light from inside growing brighter. A few strong flaps and she landed gently on the balcony railing.

No doors separated the immense room beyond from the outside. "Maybe it doesn't rain this high up," she thought. The room was richly appointed. Too rich: gold and silver everywhere.

She took flight: floating past the oversized, gold-framed mirror, and a gold desk with a large, important-looking book bound in snakeskin, equipped with a lock, keeping it safe (from whom?).

She headed down a dimly lit hallway to the adjoining rooms – all of them were gigantic. (It didn't look this big from the outside.) The first looked like the kitchens. No, it wasn't food they were cooking.

At the end of the hall was a massive wooden door. The way

down, she guessed. There was a chair by it. Odd.

The room just before the door – the bedroom, probably …

Then – something hit her. Not an object. Air? Something. She fluttered and dropped to the stone floor, losing her footing and falling over.

Something was in there. Something wrong.

Why was she here? Why did she come here? Why did she have to go in?

Her little birdy heart thumping in her breast, she took to the air, heading back out. No. No. She had to go on. Why? What was it?

She spun around. At the end of the hall, she slowly banked left into the candlelit bedchambers, the flickering wicks casting shadows on the walls.

On the far wall, lit from one side by a distant candle, a double window, stood wide open, inviting the cool night breezes to whip around the room, shaking the candle flames. There was a shape there at the window – dark against the dark night. Human? Monster? Or silhouette?

Drawing closer. No movement. The shape didn't cast a shadow of its own.

Closer still. Was it a shadow of something else? A coat, hanging? A hooded figure? Why was there no shadow?

Hovering a few feet from it, she still couldn't say for sure.

She floated around to the side, coming from the direction of the candlelight.

It was a garment. A cloak? A hood? A little closer. Her heart pounding in her ears.

Why didn't it cast a shadow? Then she stopped short.

The head turned. It was a head. Hooded. Turning. But not in her direction, thank goodness.

She froze. Oh, no. She saw it, the same second the figure did. It was her shadow on the wall. Clearly.

The head spun around, inches from her. A horrid, green face, shock-black hair, green eyes, a red open mouth screaming, "Get out!"

She screeched in horror, darting one way, then another, confused.

Large, green hands reached out, thin fingers grasping.

Where to go? Where?

The window.

Sparks flew from the tips of the green fingers, hitting the wall behind her, spewing rock.

Out the window, finally. Out and down.

Another spark cracked the air around her.

Was she hit?

Was she falling? Diving? Cold, somehow burning air rushing past her.

Down faster and faster.

Something? Something else in the distance. Faint.

"Brooke?"

Faster still.

She heard it. "Brooke." She knew that voice.

Faster. Falling. The wall. The ground. Would her wings even work?

"Brooke." Clearer now: her mother's voice.

The hard ground rushed at her.

"No!"

❀ ❀ ❀ ❀ ❀ ❀ ❀

Stillness.

Queen Jessica held her daughter, who'd grown silent. Looking to the broken King beside her, then back to her girl, she shook her head.

Brooke was no longer breathing.

The Princess melted limp, out of her mother's arms, onto the pile of pillows.

❀ ❀ ❀ ❀ ❀ ❀ ❀

Dark. So dark, she could be anywhere.

Nowhere.

Then she felt it: a cool breeze. She leaned into it, and her wings caught hold. She was soaring.

Soaring.

❀ ❀ ❀ ❀ ❀ ❀ ❀

Her lungs filled with air. Clean and fresh and ... free, air.

She let it out with a smile and a sigh.

"Oh, baby," the Queen cried out.

The King and everyone in the room let out a sigh while servants started jabbering to each other.

The King shook the old physician's hand – his other hand, wiping tears from his cheeks.

The little Princess pulled her eyes halfway open and smiled.

The smiling faces of her parents greeted her. "You're here," she said, weakly.

"Where else would we be?" her father's comforting voice answered.

She lifted her hand, and the Queen folded it gently into both of hers. "I heard you, Mother."

"I knew you would," Queen Jessica told her.

Brooke took her hand back suddenly and blinked a few times until her eyes were really open. She pushed herself up higher against the headboard, making sounds, opening and closing her mouth as everyone watched. "I'm hungry," she said in full voice.

The whole room relaxed and smiled. Princess Brooke was back.

She grabbed hold of each of her parents' hands and said, "Let's go down to the kitchens. All of us," she said including the roomful of people. "We'll sit at the kitchen table and have chef make us ... everything," she said, throwing up her arms.

"As you wish, Your Highness," the King said, standing up. He picked his little girl up in his arms. "Wake up the castle," he commanded. "Everyone."

Servant girls curtsied and ran ahead.

The Queen tucked a throw blanket around Brooke.

"We feast in the kitchens this night," the King decreed, heading for the door.

"A feast," Princess Brooke yelled out, raising her fist in the air.

Everyone cheered and laughed, joining the procession.

The Queen urged them all out the door. As their voices began to fade, her head slowly sank. She held onto the bedpost to keep from collapsing completely. Hearing her name being called, she resumed her royal posture. "Coming," she yelled into the corridor and smiled. It was a good day. They survived. Her little Princess came back from the darkness – and not for the first time ... or the last.

Pulling a lace handkerchief from somewhere in her sleeve, she dabbed each eye and followed the cheering voices.

~ *VI* ~
The Curse
(or The Spell)

T he last few miles were the worst – knowing he was close. The city spread out before him, beyond that, the walls of the castle, the gardens, and his friend. He had so much to tell her. The best thing to do was to catch the rising heat from the streets under his wings and float high above the town, away from danger.

No. It would take too long.

Instead, he came in low, banking around corners, darting through alleyways, barely clearing one shop sign, dipping under another, then over the wall.

"What a marvelous castle. Ah, the garden in bloom." A bright white blur, streaking through the colorful landscape, directly to the open window he knew would be there. Even after a year. Had it been that long?

Ben hovered just outside the open window of the sitting room. "What if she doesn't remember me? Or doesn't want me?" He'd never considered that. Not for a moment.

He could just make out the hem of a dress – the rest of her hidden in the shadows. She was waiting for him, sitting in a chair. "Reading, I'll wager," he said to himself.

He had to see her.

Darting through the upper window. "Brooke. Brooke, I'm back," he said as he back-flapped a bit, landing gently in the chair just opposite – "Oh."

It wasn't the Princess after all.

"Ah," the Queen said, setting down the book she'd been reading. "The Prodigal Bird returns."

Ben was surprised, but not so much that he forgot his manners. He tweeted, "Your Majesty," and bowed.

"You're aware, I don't understand you?" she asked him.

"Yes, Your Highness," he said, bowing again before realizing that answering her made no sense.

"Yes," she said, with a little smile, as though she knew what he was thinking. "This is a situation, rife with opportunities for misunderstanding. Let's see if we can remedy that, shall we?"

Ben nodded.

"Excellent," she said. "Just to be sure that I'm speaking to the Parakeet Prince that my daughter has spoken so highly of, I'm going to ask you to speak – or tweet, or whatever's proper – in this pattern: three tweets, a short pause, and then two additional noises." She motioned for him to begin.

Ben tweeted the pattern perfectly.

Bowing her head slightly, the Queen said, "It's a pleasure to meet you, Prince Benjamin."

"The pleasure is all mine, Your Majesty," he said, bowing. (He couldn't help it.)

"I'll do my best to ask you only yes or no questions," she told him. "I believe the most common procedure is one tweet for yes, and two for no. Is that acceptable?"

Ben tweeted once.

"Wonderful," she said with a smile and a little squeeze of her shoulders. "It's like a game, isn't it?"

Ben tweeted once.

"If you overlook the fact that you're under a spell, that is," she said, straightening the pleats in her already perfect dress. "Higginbotham, is that correct?" she asked.

One tweet.

"Rulers of Athenaeum if I recall. In the north, the far side of the Nascita Mountains, is that right?"

One tweet.

"And you were here last, just before Brooke's birthday, weren't you?" she asked with a smile.

A pause. Ben tweeted twice, cocking his head to one side, getting a better view of the Queen. She didn't seem like someone who made a lot of mistakes.

"Was it on her birthday?"

Two tweets. Without being obvious about it, he began to map out an escape route. Something was up.

"Just after."

Ben tweeted once.

"My apologies for testing you, Your Highness," she said. "I can never be too sure when it comes to my daughter's safety, particularly if there's magic involved."

Ah, that's what it was. One tweet.

She leaned in to speak to the little bird. "From the little I've seen of you, my feeling is that you can have very strong reactions to certain facts. I'm wondering if you could promise me you'll keep your emotions in check when I tell you this next bit of news?"

Oh, no. Ben was already becoming agitated. He ruffled his feathers.

"You're very important to my little girl," she told him in a calm voice. "I don't quite know how it happened so quickly, but Brooke needs you."

This made the Parakeet in Ben even more agitated.

"Prince Benjamin," she said, calmly but quite firm, "Your friend ... needs you."

Ben brought the bird in himself under control. He tweeted once with a nod of his little head.

Queen Jessica gave him a royal nod of approval. She told the Parakeet Prince of Brooke's daily and nightly vigil, waiting for his return – not to make him feel guilty but because a friend deserves the whole truth. She detailed the horrible ordeal with her fever, and how she never fully recovered. "The Princess is no longer sick," she told him, "nor is she completely well. Do you understand?"

One tweet.

"My daughter is not like ..." the Queen gave a little laugh. "I was about to say, she's not like everyone else, but the fact is, she's not like *anyone* else."

Ben tweeted twice, shaking his head.

"I'm pleased and very grateful for your return, Your Highness. I believe you're just the medicine she needs to fully recover," she told him. "Metaphorically, that is," she added quickly, "It's not as though we're going to make a stew out of you or something."

Ben gave a very loud tweet, and then continued tweeting quite a bit.

Queen Jessica assumed it was some sort of bird laughter. (It was.)

"She's resting upstairs at the moment," she said, heading for the doors. "I thought I'd take this opportunity to furnish you with the missing pieces of our story." She tugged on a velvet rope, hanging near the entrance. "Would you like that?"

One tweet.

"Oh, do you drink tea?" She looked around the room, thinking. "I'm trying to recall what I've read about budgies' eating and drinking habits?"

Ben wasn't sure either. He tweeted once. Then twice. Then shook his head.

"No matter," she said. "I'll serve some up, cooled, and we'll find out together, shall we?"

One tweet.

"I'll recite the story the same as I do to Brooke," she said, getting comfortable. "Keep you from having to compare facts later. 'Fair warning: she's a stickler for the truth, that girl."

"As am I," Ben said, and then remembered she didn't understand. He threw up his wings and dropped them in an, "I give up," gesture – Parakeet-style.

Queen Jessica did the same, only human-style. She tapped the thick, cushiony arm of her chair, offering it to Ben. "Would you like to ...?"

Ben tweeted once and flutter-hopped over to her chair.

"No need to be so formal," she said. "After all, it's storytelling."

One tweet.

❀ ❀ ❀ ❀ ❀ ❀ ❀

Romantic tales speak of broken hearts but never of the physical pain your body must endure each and every day.

I wasn't a good wife to Brooke's father, nor a good companion. It was unfair to him, yet he always treated me as the greatest gift he'd ever been given. Even after I told him of my affections for Beauregard.

❀ ❀ ❀ ❀ ❀ ❀ ❀

You know who Beau is, right?

One tweet.

"Our marriage didn't begin with love. It started with honesty, and that's a good foundation for any relationship, don't you think?"

One tweet.

❀ ❀ ❀ ❀ ❀ ❀ ❀

My parents tried to cheer me up by throwing an extravagant grand ball to celebrate our second anniversary.

The night of the ball, after the King and Queen had retired, there was a lull in the music, and I heard Beau's name being announced. My heart jumped into my throat, and I didn't know what to do or where to turn. My husband took hold of my hand and held me steady.

Beauregard's entrance to the ballroom was something to behold. It was clear he'd become a Sorcerer to reckon with. He stood atop the marble staircase, a black cloak with silver trim over his shoulders. His skin had gone from pale to a distinct green color – it was inhuman.

❀ ❀ ❀ ❀ ❀ ❀ ❀

"Oh, my word," Ben said, becoming agitated again.

The Queen only heard tweet, tweet, tweet.

"It's alright," she told him. "It's just a story."

Ben got hold of the flighty Parakeet in him.

"You were aware of his complexion, or suspected as much, didn't you?" Queen Jessica asked.

One tweet.

"Still, a bit of a shock, though."

One tweet.

The Queen stared at the little Parakeet, saying nothing. Maybe she was waiting for him to calm down. Like Ben, it was sometimes difficult to tell exactly what she was thinking. Until she smiled – that was unmistakable.

She smiled at the bird and continued ...

❀ ❀ ❀ ❀ ❀ ❀ ❀

Beau waited until the crowd's attention was focused on him, then he flung open his robes and dozens of blackbirds took flight above the crowd.

Some cowered. Some cheered.

Halfway down the stairs, Beau threw both arms in the air with a flourish, and the birds overhead exploded, becoming bits of confetti, showering the crowd with hundreds of glittering, silver coins. The guests scrambled after the money, leaving Beau an open path to the two of us.

My Prince put a hand on the hilt of his sword and stepped in front of me. "You're not welcome here, sir," he told him.

Beau laughed at him. "That's so cute," he said to me. Then back to my husband, "Are you going to protect your wife?" Then his smiled disappeared and with a simple wave of his hand, my husband was thrown into the air like a doll, crashing through the windows, out onto the balcony.

"No!" I screamed and ran toward him.

Beau grabbed my arm. "Leave him," he said. "He'll be fine. He's a big, strong Prince."

"Why must you be so hateful?" I asked him.

"Me?" he said, pretending to be insulted. "Look who's talking."

I got free of him and ran.

"Enough!" he yelled in a booming voice. The entire ballroom stopped in an instant – everyone froze in place. I tried to move my legs, but it was though they were made of stone.

"Correct me if I'm wrong, but didn't you tell me you didn't love him?" Beau said, to the statue that was me. "Isn't that what you said?"

"Let me go to him. To see if he's alright," I asked. "It's just outside."

He gave a show of thinking about it then shook his head. "No," he said and moved to within an inch of my face. "No, my lost love." Then he smiled that crooked smile. His whole being seemed crooked, as well. "You will never go outside again. Never feel the freedom you fought so hard for. No wind on your skin, no grass beneath your feet." He walked around me, explaining, "You see, I've given a great deal of thought to what I might do to make sure you couldn't go on destroying men's lives as you did mine. I must confess, I did consider killing you. Then I thought, 'I should really give you a chance. You know, for old time's sake.'"

He stopped and faced me again, "Let's see if your precious love can grow when you're stuck within these walls. What will you become without your precious freedom? My guess? You'll turn bitter and sour, or you'll simply rot."

With that, he took out his wand and aimed it at me, saying these words, "You shall never leave, come what may, remain inside, for every day."

Remembering when Brooke spoke the words, Ben finished the spell with her, "... for every day."

I felt an awful pain in the pit of my belly.

I watched, still frozen, as he returned to the top of the marble stairs and addressed the ballroom of statues. "I want to thank you all. I've had a marvelous time, but I really must fly." With that, he threw open his cloak and transformed into a large black bird.

The giant raven flapped its wings, bringing everyone in the room back to life.

I fell to the ground in pain, holding my stomach.

People were running and screaming as the massive bird swooped down over the crowd, then flew out of the broken windows and out of our lives.

❀ ❀ ❀ ❀ ❀ ❀ ❀

The Queen allowed the little bird time to take this in.

He was trying to piece it together: cocking his head one way and the other, looking back to Queen Jessica for help. Ben had never wanted to be able to talk more than he did right now. Was there more to the curse? The sorcerer didn't come back to curse the child. Does a mother pass a curse down to her child? Are they both … "Oh."

From his perch on the armchair, he looked at the Queen's belly, where she felt the pain of the curse, and then drifted up to her face.

Queen Jessica nodded, seeing that the Parakeet now understood the pain she felt that night, and guilt she carried with her every day. "Yes," she told him, "my little Princess was growing inside of me then. I wasn't aware I was pregnant at the time."

Turning toward the windows and the garden beyond, the Queen said, "I often wonder if magic is drawn toward the strongest life force. Or why he didn't name me in his curse. Why couldn't he have done that?" She shook her head.

Facing the Parakeet again, she told him, "So you see, your friend was never cursed, she merely inherited the imprisonment meant for her mother. I'm sure Beau would relish the fact his curse produced a punishment ten times more cruel than he intended."

Ben's little birdy heart was small, but he would surely offer it up to ease a mother in such pain.

"It never occurred to us that it was the baby who was under the spell and not myself. Have you seen how it works?" she asked Ben.

He tweeted once.

"Well, it was the same with me. More than a step, and I would vanish, instantly reappearing indoors. I'll admit, at first, I was crushed. My freedom was precious. When I began to feel life inside of me, she became far more dear."

Ben tweeted once. He understood.

"We were so happy," she told Ben. "Beau's curse had failed him. Remaining indoors focused my attention on my home and husband. He took on duties of the crown, due to my father's poor health, so my help was indispensable. We were seldom apart. Out of that forced intimacy, our friendship, and the impending birth of our child came a love strong enough to withstand the tests of time and trouble – even magical ones. We'd call on all of that strength the night Brooke was born."

❀ ❀ ❀ ❀ ❀ ❀ ❀

Men are spared the pain of childbirth. So, you may not fully appreciate the magnitude of a particularly difficult birth ...

It was the second day of my labor. The physician and nursemaids had been working in shifts in order to sleep and keep up their strength. Obviously, I didn't.

None of us knew we were engaged in a battle, pitting the forces of nature – my unborn child – against the unnatural powers of magic. She wanted life, but the spell was so strong it kept her from even going outside my body.

❀ ❀ ❀ ❀ ❀ ❀ ❀

"You've met my daughter; she's not someone who's easily denied."

One tweet.

❀ ❀ ❀ ❀ ❀ ❀ ❀

I was so grateful when I finally pushed her out into the world. We all were. The doctor held her up. As tears of joy began to fall ... she vanished.

I screamed so loud my husband burst into the room, fearing the worst.

"She's gone, she's gone," I cried.

"Who? What? What happened?" he demanded of the physician.

Everyone was so confused. The doctor was looking at his

hands; the blanket that held the child was empty. "I don't ... The baby was here, and then ..."

"Then, what?" he yelled.

Then, I felt her again and cried out, "She's here ... She's inside of me," I told them.

"A girl?" he asked. "We have a girl?"

"I can feel her moving."

"That's not possible," the doctor said.

"I can feel her," I yelled at him.

The physician was about to argue, but my husband demanded I be examined.

"Of course, Your Majesty," he said taking out his instrument, "But I can assure you that –" He dropped the instrument and backed away from me, shaking his head in disbelief. "It's true," he said.

A nurse fainted. Another screamed and ran from the room.

Regaining his senses, the doctor said, "She ... the baby ... won't be able to breathe." Then he yelled to the remaining nurse, "We must get the child out, now."

"Out," Brooke's father said to himself. "No. Wait."

Everyone stopped. He leaned close, "Do you trust me, Jessica?"

"Completely," I said.

"Follow me," he told the others and unlatched the balcony doors. "Bring the bed. Bring everything," he demanded, pushing the doors open. A rush of cool air sent the curtains flying.

Together, they pushed the bed with me in it to the doorway.

He positioned the bed so that my legs were outside – but the rest of my body remained indoors. "Get the child out, now," he told the doctor.

I reached for his hand, pulling him to me. "I can't," I told him, "Please, no. It's too much." To go through the pain of childbirth again, right after ... I was so weak.

He took me in his arms and held me. "I love you, Jessica," he whispered in my ear. "You must save our daughter."

I nodded, took in a deep breath of the night air, dug my fingers into his back and pushed and pushed and pushed her out into the world again, on a balcony under the stars. The instant the doctor took hold of Brooke, my Prince dragged the bed back inside.

Once more, she vanished.

My girl reappeared, wet and warm on the cushion of my belly.

The doctor cut her loose, and she cried loud enough to shatter glass.

❀ ❀ ❀ ❀ ❀ ❀ ❀

"This girl challenged the forces of magic and bested them. She did so as a mere infant in the womb," the Queen told the little bird on the arm of her chair. "She hasn't stopped in that effort, nor will she. As a woman, I fear the stakes for doing so will increase, along with the dangers."

Ben nodded, more to himself.

"You have an idea of what the future might hold, don't you?"

He couldn't see how it would be possible, but ... He tweeted once.

"I can't know what winds of change brought you here, Prince Benjamin of Athenaeum," she said, pulling his attention back to her. "By chance or design, you are bound to my daughter. More importantly, you've become her friend."

One tweet.

"As such, you must find the means to quell whatever bird tendencies you have that would lead you to fly away in times of trouble. If you can't do so, you must leave. Brooke might survive without the love and support of a good friend, but she couldn't bear being abandoned by one."

She waited to make sure Ben understood.

"Not an easy relationship, by any means," she said with a smile. "I'm sure you're aware you can't put a price on friendship, especially with one whose heart is as open as the sky. Otherwise, you wouldn't have come back."

One tweet.

"I wanted to be sure you know, in this case, there is a cost. It's bravery, loyalty, devotion, and the belief that anything is possible."

Ben nodded his little head.

"We scour the earth and heavens for signs of a miracle. Brooke is living proof."

~ *VII* ~

Home

The first four times he flew away from the castle there was no doubt in his mind: to stay meant risking his life.

He flew back with the same conviction, even hopping onto a branch of the young tree peeking through the skylight. To leave would dishonor his family, his name, his position.

The last few times back and forth weren't so clear. He couldn't tell if his fowl instincts were demanding he take flight while his conscience insisted he stay.

Perched on a wooden crossbeam of the glass roof, he wondered if there was anything more foolish than a bird, standing only six inches tall, believing himself to be a hero? Or if there was anything smaller than a man who wouldn't stand by a friend in need?

The one thing he hadn't done on any of his round-trip flights was take a moment to look at her. Until now.

It was clear why he hadn't.

One look at Brooke's face, and he knew he could never leave her. He would sacrifice his life for her in a minute. A minute with her was more rewarding than a lifetime with anyone else on earth.

Prince Benjamin flew into his friend's room and perched on the footboard of her large bed. He watched her restless sleep. The year had changed her. The soft edges of her features were a bit more defined; she was thinner, probably taller.

"Good evening, Your Highness," he said to her.

Without opening her eyes, she smiled and stretched out her arms. "Ben," she said, just above a whisper.

Perhaps she was still dreaming.

"At your service," he said.

She opened her eyes a little. "I love the way you talk." She finished her stretch and bounced up to a sit, wide awake. "What took you so long?"

"It's a long story, Your Highness."

"Hmm," she said, looking at him a bit sideways. "First of all, stop with the, 'your highness,' stuff. Second of all, I happen to love long stories."

As Ben opened his mouth to speak, Brooke added, "Third of all, you don't have to tell me anything, if you don't want, or until you do want to. Because, fourth of all, I'm just so happy to have you back, Benjamin."

The little bird cocked his head to one side and then the other, allowing each eye to gaze on the Princess. "Strange ..." he said, letting the word hang in the air.

"What is?"

He cocked his head once more to be sure, saying, "You've been confined to this castle for all your days and quite ill recently, I've been told, yet I can't find a hint of sorrow in your face – and my eyesight is exceptional, by the way. While I've sung only sad songs for the past few years, and I'm ... well, free as a bird."

"How can I mourn, when the next time I open my eyes, there could be a Prince at my bedside?" she asked, smiling.

"Oh, I missed you, Princess," he said.

"Not nearly as much as I missed my only and bestest friend," she told him.

Brooke scooted down to the bottom of the bed to be closer to him. She let the smile wander from her lips, "I never had a friend. Someone I could ... Hmm," she thought about it for a moment. "I'm exceptionally lucky ..."

Ben nodded her along.

"And I truly believe anything is possible. It's just that ... everyone's so worried about me being sad. I don't want to disappoint them, you know?" she said.

"I do," he said.

She let herself relax a bit and leaned against the footboard. "I can't tell them ... There are times when I can't stop myself from thinking how unfair it all is. Mom would feel so guilty if she knew I'd cried myself to sleep. Not often," she added. Brooke straightened a fold in her nightgown and smoothed it out. "I've spent hours gazing out the window, watching people, just gardening. Picking a flower ... Sometimes I ache to be like everyone else ..." She looked at the little bird and scratched his chest with her finger. Smiling again, "But you know what? Those are only passing pains. If I stare out a window long enough, I start to see it all with a touch of my mother's sight: I know those people labor day and night, some aching with real pain, crying themselves to sleep with empty bellies. I'm a Princess, for heaven's sake," she said, sitting up straight again. "I don't have the right to feel sorry for myself. In fact, it's shameful for me to ever complain."

"Not shameful," he told her, "... human." He swiped her nose lightly with an open wing.

"Yeah," she said.

"It's I who should be ashamed," he said.

"Don't be silly. You've been forced to live in a body not your own. Spent years alone with no one to talk to. You have every reason to be upset." Then she smiled. "Until now, that is." Brooke clapped her hands together, barely able to contain her excitement. "Don't you feel as though the most unexpected things are always happening? You can't wait to see what surprises might be around the next corner?"

"No, not really."

"Oh," she said, slumping her shoulders.

"I never thought I was particularly special in any way, until, well ... this," he said, opening his wings to give her the full bird view.

"You're a Prince," she pointed out. "You have to admit – that's kinda special."

"Not so much in my family. I'm the youngest of seven brothers. Even if Fate twisted itself into a pretzel, I'd never be King," he said, hopping onto the bed cover as Brooke lay down. "I wasn't a very good Prince," he admitted. "Oh, I can – could – handle a sword and steed pretty well. I enjoyed reading about great battles and developing strategies – but combat itself not so much. A bit more of a Parakeet, then a Prince, I'm afraid," he said, throwing in a little laugh (which, to anyone else would sound like a couple of chirps: instead of, "Haha," they'd hear, "Chirpchirp," which would make no sense at all).

He took a few birdy steps closer until he stood face to face with the Princess, then told her, solemnly, as though admitting some terrible character flaw: "The truth is, I spent most of my time in the library, surrounded by books."

"I see," Brooke said, nodding; doing her best to take the adorable little bird's heartfelt confession seriously, when what she wanted to do was smother him with kisses. Then she whispered, as though someone might be listening, "I'm the same. We have an excellent library. I've spend days in it, and nights – reading by candlelight till it's light again." Then she laughed. "How silly of that Sorcerer to think he could keep us in prison when we've got keys to unlock the universe between the covers of every book."

Brooke was out of bed and running to her dressing room. Yelling back, "I'll get dressed while you tell me all about your travels."

Taking flight, Ben said, "I thought you said I didn't have to tell you anything until I wanted to?"

Brooke turned around at the dressing room door. "Well, don't you want to?" she asked.

"I suppose so," he said, coming to rest on the tea table.

"Well, there you go," she said. "Start squawking." And she disappeared into her dressing room, leaving the door open a crack.

"Where should I start?" Ben said to himself, organizing his thoughts.

"Good question," Brooke said from behind the door. "Most people like to start at the beginning. 'I began life as a small egg.' Haha. Me? I like to skip around. Keep things interesting. Oh, I know." She peeked out the door. "Start with, where you went after falling from the Sorcerer's tower?"

Ben stepped back, "What did you say?"

Behind the door again. "After we fell from the tower, I lost you. My fever broke, and I wasn't with you anymore. Strange. Why do you think that was?"

Ben's feathers ruffled. He shook out his wings. What was happening?

"Or why you went there in the first place. I knew you would, still ..." she said, coming out, lacing up the front of her dress. "Why did you go there?"

She spotted him on the table, pacing around. He knocked into a teacup.

"Ben, what is it? What's wrong?"

"How could you know that?" Ben said. He flapped his wings,

knocking more of the tea set around.

She bent down, closer to his level. "It's alright. It's alright. Nothing to worry about," she said calmly. "No reason to get flighty."

"I don't ... I can't ..." And he flew up in the air.

"Don't leave me. No," she cried.

The Parakeet was darting back and forth and took off toward the apple tree and the opening in the ceiling.

"Don't you leave me again, please," she begged.

There it was, up ahead. The sky. The air. He could breathe again.

"Please."

He circled the tree. He could feel the cool, fresh air. He was about to push up and out and be free when he heard a 'thump.' He swung around again to see Brooke had dropped to her knees, her head hanging.

She looked as though she was about to cry. Instead, she began shaking her head back and forth, slowly. No, no, no, she would not let the tears fall. She took a deep breath and shook it all off, lifting her head to see her friend. "I have no right to ask you to stay," she said. "To share a prison when you're free to roam the skies."

The flutter of his wings slowed.

"If, and when, you'd like to return, you know you're always welcome. I'll be here," she said. She laughed. "Of course. Silly me. I can't leave."

Ben settled on the edge of the planter.

"It was lovely to see you, Ben," she said, getting to her feet. "I'm sorry if I upset you."

Ben glided over to her. "I should be the one apologizing," he said.

"Oh. Okay," she said. "Go ahead."

"Uh ... alright," he said, gathering his thoughts. "I'm so sorry, Brooke. Too often, I give in to the baser instincts of this creature I'm trapped in when it's my heart and mind that should rule. I will allow it no longer. From this day forward, I promise to remain by your side, for as long as you'll have me."

They looked at each other in silence. The Princess and the Parakeet.

Brooke said to him, "You should apologize more often. You're really good at it."

"I shall," he said. "Whenever necessary."

"You should just throw it in, anytime," she said. "Oh, look. You knocked over the tea set. I'm really upset about that. You should probably say you're sorry."

She laughed, and he chirped.

"If I haven't said so yet ... Wait, have I?" She thought about it. Then waved it away. "Welcome home, Ben."

He bowed, saying, "Thank you, Brooke. It's good to be home."

"It does feel like this is where you belong, doesn't it?"

"More than any place I've been," he told her. "Even the place I was born."

"Oh, was it horrible?" she asked. "Did your mother disown you? Did your father beat you?"

"What? No."

"That's a shame," she said. "It'd be a much more interesting story if they did, don't you think?" Before he could answer, "Oh, I know. Tell me what happened after we fell from the tower. Wait, you're not going to get all 'flighty' again, are you?"

"No, I'm calm," he told her. "About that. How could you know?"

"I was with you. Didn't you feel me?" He shook his head. "No? Think back, Ben. On the road, before you ever got to the forest? Before you knew what it was? Didn't you feel something?"

"There was ... But how could that be?"

"No 'how' now," she said, waving the idea off. "Did you know about the petals of the monster flower? That they could hide you and not crush you when they folded up at night? Do you know very much about flowers?" He shook his head. "Well, I do. With the giant mosquito, did you know your beak was powerful enough to tear its body into pieces? I did. I looked it up. Your beak is really strong."

"You ... were there," he said, figuring it out. "It's impossible."

"Lots of things are until you do them."

Ben said, "I can't say for sure ..."

"You mean, you won't."

"This is something beyond reason," he told her. "You can't present it as factual."

"Or, you won't."

He shook his head. He was trying to make her understand, "A 'feeling' by definition is an emotion, and therefore cannot be–"

"Will not be."

"Scientifically measured."

"By you," she added.

"You're infuriating," he told her.

"Don't get your feathers all ruffled just because you're wrong," she said, smiling.

"I am not ..." he started to say, but gave up. "Alright, I felt you were with me."

"Really? Are you sure?" she asked. Then laughed. "Wasn't it wonderful? Wasn't it marvelous? Wasn't it the most exciting thing? Except when we were scared out of our wits and in danger of being killed – which was most of the time. You're so brave. I never would've risked my life like that."

"It seems as though you already have," he said.

"Oh. Right," she said. "Why did you?

"First off, I wasn't aware the forest had become ..."

"Evil," she said, helping.

"Yes, I suppose so," he said. "Evil. I'd picked up rumors, here and there, nothing that could've prepared me for that," he said. "I had to be certain the Sorcerer was still alive – no one knew. If he was, I thought there was a chance he might listen to reason. If he was made aware you'd been unjustly imprisoned by his curse—"

"It's a spell, but go on," Brooke said.

"Well, he might consider lifting it. The spell," Ben finished. "Obviously not. It was ridiculous for me to think I could—"

"No it wasn't," Brooke interrupted. "It was incredibly brave, and kind, and extraordinary."

"Well, I ..." he said. "Anyway, after the fall from the tower, my wing was in fairly bad shape."

"Wait. What happened?" Brooke asked. "We didn't hit the ground. The last thing I remember was soaring."

"That's correct," he said. "But coming out of the fall, the speed we were traveling put too much strain on my right wing. I was unable to fly for several weeks. Fortunately, I landed within the castle grounds."

"You didn't cross the forest again?" Brooke asked.

"Perhaps you'd better sit," he suggested.

"Oh, no," she said.

"This tiny frame isn't built to fly over the mountains; however, the wood doesn't stretch quite as far heading toward the capital," he explained. "I wasn't certain I could make it in a day's time, but it was the lesser of two evils if you'll excuse the pun. As it turned out, I couldn't. I was growing weak as the sun inched closer to the horizon, bringing me closer to the roof of the forest."

"Oh, my," Brooke said.

"I could hear the night creatures coming to life below. My hopes lifted when I thought I saw the end of the forest. Then it became clear it was a patch of forest – set apart somehow – and the wood spread for miles beyond it. The shadow demons began to crash through the top of the canopy into the twilight. I darted this way and that, avoiding them. None were emerging from the grove ahead. The mosquitos would be next, so I pushed harder."

"Just then, I heard the terrible, piercing cry of some misshapen monster in the sky above. I spotted a dark four-winged beast. Diving straight at me. Its jaw stretched wide, white fangs catching the last rays of sun, its scream drawing the other hungry fowl. Enormous mosquitos popped up in every direction as I grew closer to the grove. The beast was bearing down. Dark shapes joining the chase. I dipped over and under the giant insects as they joined the pack. Closer. But they were gaining. A sky full of black shapes with glowing eyes were on my tail. I wouldn't make it. I dropped down into the jungle - the tearing, crashing sounds of the pack in hot pursuit."

"Then a thunderous mash of screeches and howls, bones shattering. Followed by silence. I found myself surrounded by straight, solid trees – no vines or deformed creature in sight. I'd arrived in the grove. I slowed down and turned to see what became of my pursuers. The grove was some kind of wall, barring their entrance. The beasts had crashed into it. Mangled bodies, talons, and wings struggling in a pile of the dead and dying. Dozens of scavengers were already descended on them, ripping the meat from their bones, many still breathing."

Ben turned to Brooke, sitting there, her eyes wide open. "What was the grove?" she asked him.

"I don't know. There was a warmth to it I can't explain. At its center, a circle with no trees at all. I roosted for the night and cleared the forest by noon the next day."

"I realize a bird's eye view of one's home is nothing like your childhood memories, but the castle had changed in other ways.

Absent, was the familiar commotion of a household of princes. Serious. Sad perhaps."

"They miss you," Brooke suggested.

"I don't know," Ben said. "After so many years? My two eldest brothers weren't present. I listened in on conversations, to discover their whereabouts, or what might explain the somber mood. In fact, I was so intent on hearing an exchange between my parents, I never saw the kitchen maid come up behind me. She threw a blanket over me and locked me in a birdcage."

"Oh no," Brooke said.

"I would've returned no matter what the obstacles, but having been given a taste of the imprisonment you live every day doubled my resolve."

"My poor Ben," she said. "How did you escape?"

"More from a loss of will than ingenuity, I'm afraid," he told her. "I normally wouldn't share this type of information–"

"But it's me."

"But it's you, so … The prospect of living out my days in a prison, mute to my loving family, steps away, became too much for me. I didn't care to eat or drink. After a time, I lay on the floor of the cage, hoping the end would come."

Brooke's hands covered her mouth.

"When the kitchen maid discovered me, she began wailing and blubbering, on and on. 'What to do?' How she's lost her only friend. (I spared you the torture of this woman's ceaseless chattering. It may have contributed more to my suicidal tendencies than being incarcerated. I now know far too much about the inner workings of the castle kitchens. If we should ever find ourselves at my ancestral home, please, whatever we do, we must not eat the soup.) Imagining me at death's door, the maid gathered me up and set my limp body on her pillow as she fashioned a funnel in order to force-feed me. I knew this because the woman narrated her entire life: every action and thought in her head. Not so near to my last breath as either of us thought, I simply got up and flew out the window. She probably went on with her monolog for twenty minutes more before realizing her audience had fled."

"And from there you came home to me," she said, smiling.

"Directly, Princess," he said.

"Yay. Happy ending," she pointed out. "I'm starving. Are you hungry? It's late, isn't it? For you, I mean. You're used to roosting at dusk. Haha. 'Used to roosting,'" she repeated. "You must be exhausted."

"I must admit, I am," he said.

"Oh," she said and sprung out of her chair. She looked back at Ben as she crossed to the far side of her bed, to what looked like a large piece of furniture covered with a sheet.

Ben flew to the footboard.

Brooke slumped. "Oh. I'm not sure it's so wonderful after your last adventure." She straightened up and said, "I hope you'll accept this gift in the manner of ... I'm not good at this stuff. Here," she said, pulling the sheet off.

Beneath was a giant golden birdcage. Various perches throughout, a swing, dishes filled with all kinds of nuts and seeds, and an ornate (yet masculine) birdbath in the center. A good portion of the front of the metal frame had been removed to leave a wide opening. There were open spaces on both sides and the back.

"No doors," Brooke said quietly, trying to gauge his reaction. He was so hard to read sometimes.

"'You think it's a place you might want to roost?"

"Very much," Ben told her. "It's exquisite ... perfect. Thank you," he said, barely able to speak. He cleared his little birdy throat and said, "In fact, do you mind?"

"By all means," she said, giving him room. "Roost away."

Ben swooped into his new home, landing lightly on one of the perches and trying it out, grabbing it with his toes. "Very nice," he said, and then hopped over to another, slightly thicker piece of wood, testing that. "Oh, yes," he said.

Right away, he began preening. Taking off, he flew around the cage, landing in the same spot. Repeating the actions again. Once more. His movements slowed and slowed until they became nothing at all.

Brooke sat on her bed, resting her head on her arms, leaning on the footboard, watching her friend sleep.

That's how the King found her nearly an hour later when he quietly opened the door.

Brooke smiled at him as he made his way over to the bed and settled in next to her.

He sat with her for a while. She liked this about him. Being quiet. Nothing expected.

He whispered, "How's your friend settling in?"

"He's doing the best he can under such harsh conditions," she whispered back, smiling. Settling back into her dad.

"We should get you some food, Princess."

"Aww," she said, making a face.

"I could bring it up to you," he told her.

"Would you?" she said. "I don't want to leave him. I don't think he's slept peacefully for a very long time."

"You're probably right," he said. "I can't imagine." He gave her a peck on the head. "Be back in a few," he said. He took a couple steps toward the door before something stopped him.

Brooke took her eyes off the sleeping Parakeet Prince and turned toward her dad. He was working out something. Something important. He didn't spend time on anything that wasn't.

"It's so nice and peaceful; I don't want to spoil it," he said. "It can wait."

"Dad," was all she had to say.

He came back and sat down on the bed. Talking low, "I was curious about Prince Benjamin's family, the history and such of Athenaeum, in particular how it might pertain to us."

"Uh-huh," Brooke said, nodding.

"Well, I did some digging ..."

"Uh-huh," she said, looking at him sideways.

"It seems that the Higginbothams are quite diligent about recording what transpires within their borders."

Brooke's eyes lit up.

"Which they release to the public every few years."

Brooke grabbed his arm. "And you have it?"

"Well, I had a scribe copy the entire document," he told her. "At no small expense, mind you."

"Is it here?" she asked, shaking his arm. "Does it say what happened to Ben?"

"It doesn't," he told her.

"Oh."

"It does cover events leading up to it, though. Some in Ben's own hand," the King said. "When he had hands, that is."

"I have to see. Can I read it? Please?"

"You're sure you wouldn't rather relax and spend a couple of days with your friend?" he asked. "History isn't going anywhere."

"I'm sure," she said, patting his arm, but in her mind, she'd already moved on. She got up and looked around the room, searching. "Could you have someone come and light the fire, Father?"

"At once, Your Highness," the King said, bowing.

Brooke turned to see him and smiled.

"Thank you, Father," she said because he understood her so well. "Thank you," she said again because he took such good care of her.

Remembering, "Oh, some strong tea, as well," she said after him. Adding a, "please," but he'd already gone, and she'd already moved onto something else.

She took in the beauty of her room. This was what it was designed for: a canopy of stars above, the tea table, the fireplace, a throw in case her bare calves got chilly, a large, plump armchair she could crawl up into, the long, plush couch when she wanted to stretch out.

"Now," she said, rubbing her hands together, "... something to read."

~ VIII ~

Athenaeum

She started on the floor, of all places.

On the thick hearthrug using the sofa as a backrest, her meal spread out around the edges of the large book, on the low table between her and the fire. She'd grab bites while skimming through the book, searching for anything of interest.

It wasn't really a book. A few hundred handwritten pages of large parchment paper sandwiched between two thin pieces of leather acting as the covers, tied together with a leather cord. It was mostly dates of decrees, orders, bill-of-sales for property, births, and deaths. "In the kingdom of Athenaeum, the province of something-or-other, the hamlet of such-and-such, on this, the thirteenth day of blah-blah-blah."

Pages and pages of them.

The notations by the sheriff were more interesting: a rash of thefts, a border guard abandoning his post – found later, wandering the woods, a brawl in the meat market involving pig's feet, a farmer accusing his neighbor of witchcraft in the failure of his crops, accidents, but not what she was looking for.

A complaint by a wealthy landowner in the West Country about unlawful construction on his property, just north of the Promena forest.

Brooke clamped her teeth down on the bread she was holding, freeing her hands to lift the book along with her onto the couch. Searching. Flipping a page.

Here: an entry from the West Country magistrate. Blah-blah-blah sent clerk someone-or-another to investigate ... Reported that construction had taken place. And was now completed. A stone wall of enormous proportions, standing higher than the tallest tree. No door or entrance of any kind discovered. Beyond the wall, a single castle tower rising to the heavens. Approximate estimate of time, manpower, and materials needed to construct viewable structures: twenty-five to thirty years, a minimum of one thousand laborers, and stone equaling the size of the mountain peaks to the north and east.

"Haha. I like this," she said out loud, reading: *"Due to clerk what's-his-name's propensity toward spirits, a second clerk was dispatched."* She sat up. *"Confirming the former clerk's findings. Adding, the only person seen in or around the grounds of the fortress was that of a lone figure on the tower balcony, attired in black robes."*

Below that was a lengthy entry from the king.

Brooke was shaking with excitement. She wanted to wake up Ben and say, "It's your dad. I'm reading stuff your dad wrote."

She didn't. She took a drink of tea, leaned her head back on the arm of the couch and read ...

❀ ❀ ❀ ❀ ❀ ❀ ❀

In part, due to the odd nature of the previous entries involving the unlawful construction on deeded property in the West Country, and in part to the unnatural events that follow, I, King Reginald Higginbotham, do hereby swear to the authenticity – either as an eye-witness myself, or attesting to the strength of character of those in my charge – of all that is written here by mine own hand, and scribed by my son, Prince Benjamin Mordecai Higginbotham, in my stead.

Unpracticed in the formal vernacular of the law, my son and I will record our stories here as we would speak them plainly.

Two and a half years ago, I commanded the grand sheriff of Athenaeum to begin compiling information from local magistrates and clergy, along with reports from border patrols, scouts, and royal guards, on the unlawful crossing of our border and the subsequent travels of a suspicious, male stranger of unknown origins, who displayed unnatural powers and an unnatural skin tone.

Brooke gasped.

Approximately one year ago, this stranger eluded two royal scouts in the vicinity of the southeast border of the Promena wood. We received no reports on his whereabouts since that time.

After being informed of the magistrate's investigation into the construction in the western territory and speaking in person to the clerks who reported the findings, we are acting under the assumption that the stranger and the occupant of the castle tower are one and the same, and that they may possess some form of unnatural power: magic, sorcery, witchery or the like.

To confirm or debunk these assumptions, I have dispatched an envoy to seek out the ruler of the fortress, to pay my respects and extend an invitation to visit us here, at his convenience. If he is a sorcerer with the power to construct castle grounds of that magnitude from thin

air, it seems the best course of action is to befriend him.
I also purchased the lands in and around the fortress
and the adjoining woods to avoid the possibility of land
disputes.

Brooke skipped ahead a few pages to the King's next entry some months later.

It has been several months since our envoy returned
from his assignment, failing to make contact, and
confirming the wall contained no door, gate, or entryway
of any kind visible to the naked eye. In a concerted effort
to contact the stranger, I have dispatched the following
with the subsequent results:

Dispatched: carrier pigeons, bearing invitations
and letters of introduction. Result: the birds fell from
exhaustion unable to reach their destination.

Dispatched: the kingdom's strongest archers, armed
with velvet-tipped arrows, invitations and letters of
introduction attached to the shafts. Result: missiles
managed only to clear the top of the exterior wall.

Contact with the stranger is essential. We can't know
if he poses a threat to the kingdom until we learn his
identity, the extent of his powers, and his intentions. We
must find a way to overcome a seemingly impenetrable
wall.

Ruling out the use of force – an unprovoked attack would only ensure him as an enemy – we will assemble an army consisting of the brightest minds in the kingdom: master builders, architects, inventors, and philosophers.

Brooke searched that page and another till she found the next entry.

Our fifth day – camped outside the stranger's stronghold. Flying a white flag of peace. Architects, master builders and inventors have studied and measured every foot of the great stone wall, searched for hidden entryways and weaknesses – concluding a structure this tall would need to be so thick with a foundation so deep it could never be breached.

The philosophers examined all documents regarding the stranger and the structure, consulted the builders, trekked up the mountains, dug up the road, then sat down to discuss their findings: builders confirmed the clerk's estimate; construction would take over twenty-five years, require a thousand laborers, and the equivalent of a mountain of stone; Royal Scouts searched this land one and half years prior, pursuing the stranger; there were no signs of construction, a labor force, or materials, no reports of the movement of a large labor force or stone; nearby mountains are undisturbed, and the road showed no evidence of moving that amount of stone.

Their conclusion: the wall was not built by men. The wall does not consist of stone. A power operating outside the laws of nature created the wall, using unnatural materials. Therefore, the architects, builders and inventors conclusion was incorrect: the wall doesn't obey the laws of physics or mathematics and wouldn't need a foundation at all.

Their suggestion was to dig a hole a few feet down at the base of the wall. Dig a few feet forward and then up.

I ordered a hole to be dug, and it opened up inside the wall.

I insisted that I go in alone. I came out of the hole to find a young man sitting on a golden throne facing me, wearing a hooded cloak. It was immediately clear why he'd chosen to hide from the world in a high tower behind a giant wall ...

The skin on his face and hands was a gruesome shade of green.

❀ ❀ ❀ ❀ ❀ ❀ ❀

"I knew it. I knew it," Brooke blurted out loud. Springing up, she was about to yell, "I told you," to Ben over the back of the couch, then remembered he was sleeping. So she whispered, "I told you," instead.

She knew it. They were meant to find each other. This was proof. Written proof. Her fingers lightly run over the words: *"The skin on his face and hands was a gruesome shade of green."* She wouldn't find him gruesome. She knew him too well. Beauregard. Beau. Was it so strange that she had no bitterness toward him? Poor Beau. Tortured. Alone, in his tower, behind his great wall.

"Ow." Brooke's fingers jumped back. Something stung her. Cut her? She opened her clenched fist to see. The tips were blackened. Curious, she rubbed them lightly with her thumb. The dark shadows faded away, returning her skin to its natural color.

Brooke picked up the book to examine the words on the page. No, nothing. She floated her fingers just above the words, afraid to actually touch them. There was heat coming off the page, just from that one sentence.

Was she imagining it? Was she dreaming?

"Alright," Brooke said to herself. She pulled the purple ribbon from her hair, laid it across the page as a bookmark, and set the book on the table. The fire was going nicely. Did someone come in and tend to it?

Crossing to her tea table, she lifted the cozy over the teapot and tapped it gently. Yep, it was hot. "Either some very industrious gnomes are looking out for me, or very quiet servants," she thought, as she made herself a cup of tea.

"Chair time," she decided after tea. She tied up her hair with the ribbon and settled in.

Nope. No heat coming from the words anymore ...

❀ ❀ ❀ ❀ ❀ ❀ ❀

He treated me to an extravagant feast and assured me his motives were purely peaceful. We talked for hours, touring the empty, enormous castle and grounds. I returned, day after day.

He was stingy with details of his childhood: orphaned by age six, homeless, eating from garbage, he survived using his quick tongue and nimble fingers. Destined for prison or an early grave, he found redemption in a piece of fruit and a young girl's voice. He'd climbed the high wall of an estate to swipe an apple from the rich man's orchard when he heard singing. He saw the nobleman's daughter playing alone, acting out fantasies of a thrilling life beyond the wall. He was back the next day, looking for valuables he could easily grab and easily pawn – he told himself. Then every day after, watching her plan other thrilling escapes. One of these days, he would risk his life to free her. He would be her hero. When he approached her at last, it set off a decade of unexpected adventures and deep friendship, enriching their lives in every way. He learned to read and write, how to speak and behave like a nobleman – which led to an apprenticeship with an old sorcerer. He described the love that grew between them at length and oddly: as though a spirit of their own creation possessed them. So committed to each other, body and soul, their two hearts beat as one.

News of her impeding, arranged marriage left the Sorcerer with a useless, empty heart. In a desperate attempt to change his fortune, he swallowed a potion, poisoning his skin. Jealousy filled his vacant heart, dying his infected pigment green, twisting his mind toward revenge. He couldn't bring himself to take her life, so he took back the gift he'd given her instead: her freedom.

His turn to dark magic broke his master's heart, and the young Sorcerer couldn't find a spell to mend it or erase the look of disappointment on his mentor's face, so he banished himself. Bringing him to Athenaeum.

My heart went out to the tortured magician.

When it came time for me to leave, I thanked my host and invited him to visit the castle anytime. Should he ever wish to alter his skin tone, he might use his power to help others – doing good breeds goodness. Of course, it would require a door.

The Sorcerer thanked me, pledging his help, should I need it.

Turning to go, I saw the hole had been filled in, and there was a door in the wall. Outside, I found two barrels of silver coins waiting for me: a parting gift from my new friend.

I left the door open behind me. It wouldn't be long till someone saw it as an invitation to go in.

❁ ❁ ❁ ❁ ❁ ❁ ❁

The King's entry ended there. Brooke searched the page, and the next, and next, turning page after page, getting more anxious each time.

Finally. A decree by the King, awarding plots of land adjoining the Sorcerer's castle to laborers willing and able to clear and farm the land.

Here and there reports of land bequeathed to this person and that person, this family and that. Boring.

She started biting her lip when she saw the end of the book was near.

More deeds.

"Please, please, please, please, please, please, please," she said under her breath. Her finger ran through each new entry, making sure not to miss anything, saying to herself, "Who cares about the stupid tax collection?" and "Nobody wants to know about your dumb old missing cows."

With only two pages remaining, she sighed, relieved.

❀ ❀ ❀ ❀ ❀ ❀ ❀

I, Prince Benjamin Mordecai Higginbotham ...

"Aww," Brooke said. Whispering toward the cage, "It's you. This is you." Then she went back to the book, full of smiles.

... in continuation of the reports concerning the actions of the West Country Sorcerer, I do hereby swear to the authenticity of all entries written in my hand.

The following summation is based on authenticated reports: Within six months of the King's departure, two domestics arrived at the castle seeking employment, which the Sorcerer granted. This encouraged more applications and hiring of housekeeping staff and groundskeepers, which then enticed craftsmen, tradesmen, and – with the King's generous gifting of land – farmers and the like, to set up shop. The Sorcerer has chosen to remain in his tower behind locked doors, ordering any business dealings to be left at his doorstep at night, addressed, and returned the following morning.

I witnessed the makings of a thriving village in the lands surrounding the fortress at my arrival.

My desire to visit began the moment the King told

of it. It wasn't the opulence that attracted me. It was the never-before-seen papers and manuscripts on mystical phenomena his library might contain that attracted me. At the finish of my studies, the King – with the Sorcerer's blessing – bestowed on me the honor of being the castle's first librarian. (For brevity, the West Country Sorcerer's library exceeded expectations.)

"*'For brevity.'* You're so cute," Brooke said out loud.

Reading: *A beautiful maiden with hair of gold visited me in the library. Her name was Julianna.*
"You scoundrel," Brooke said.

She had been in service since birth and never learned to read or write. Would I teach her?

"Yeah, right," Brooke commented.

I considered the possibility that her motive for tutoring was merely a way to get close to me,

"You think?"

... but it was obvious that her heart was somewhere else.

"Oh."

She wanted to learn, so she could one day read to the Sorcerer.

Her duty was to collect all business addressed for the Sorcerer in a box, deliver it, and retrieve the responses in the morning. Strict instructions to leave the box outside his door, knock, then immediately make her exit down the stairs. She followed her orders meticulously. Until one evening ...

Julianna was two flights down, after her delivery, when she discovered an urgent document in the pocket of her apron. Knowing she'd be fired for not delivering the item, she rushed back.

The moment she reached the door, it opened. Surprised at first, the Sorcerer collected the box while she stood frozen with fear. "Is that for me?" he asked, pointing to the item in her trembling hands. She nodded. He gently removed the document, thanked her, and closed his door. Now, I know nothing of love ...

"Me neither," Brooke said.

... but from her description of him, his eyes, in particular, it was clear she loved this man.

She expected to be fired. When she wasn't, she set about winning the heart of the man who'd captivated hers.

"Aww, Ben," Brooke said. "You've got some romance in you, don't you?"

Juliana was the perfect student. Within a year, she was borrowing books from the library. Fiction. At night, she would take one back up the tower, sit outside the Sorcerer's door and read aloud. Never knowing if he was listening. Night after night, on the floor, leaning against the heavy door, by candlelight – hoping against hope he was on the other side, hearing her profess her love with each inflection of her voice.

I can't say for certain if Julianna's words inspired the Sorcerer to venture out of his room, but he did. Gradually engaging people, then assisting them physically and metaphysically. In time, his green color faded, taking on a healthy bronze tone from his time in the sun.

One night, as Julianna closed the book after hours of reading, she heard the turn of a lock. The door opened, and the young Sorcerer held out his hand to her. "You have brought me back from the abyss, my lady. I owe you my life," he said.

As I write, wedding plans are being made. I can attest, there is nothing more life affirming than a happy magician. Flowers bloom in winter. This will be my last entry. I am messengering this record, and wedding invitations to the royal family and court, along with a personal request from a grateful friend: would the King do the honor of giving away the bride.

❀ ❀ ❀ ❀ ❀ ❀ ❀

Brooke stretched and yawned. She squinted at the ceiling, showing the first signs of morning. The fire in embers. "Good," she said, as sleep quickly claimed her. "Ben doesn't like fire."

~ *IX* ~

The Library

he fluttering and flapping of tiny wings was the next sound heard in the room an hour later. Ben shook himself awake and took in his surroundings. He hopped down and helped himself to a drink of cool water. "Why not," he said to himself, spotting a bowl of seeds. He cracked one open with his beak and finagled the tasty meat into his craw. Delicious. He'd be back for more.

First, he wanted to check on his sleeping Princess. Odd. The bed was turned down ...

The smell of charcoal caused him to swing around in midair. He spied the ashes in the fireplace. Okay. No fire. Oh, there she was. Curled up on the couch: a soft blanket barely covering her legs. Some enormous, loose-bound book open on the table. "Fell asleep, reading by the fire, did you?" he tweeted quietly.

Just when he thought there was no way he could imagine her

more precious than he already did, she found a way.

It took a few tries to hook the blanket in his beak. Once wrangled, he dragged it up and up, letting it float down over her shoulders. Pleased with his tucking-in abilities, he strutted along the arm of the sofa to get a better look at the massive manuscript.

Ben flapped his wings and tried to shake himself awake again. He took off fast and swept wide around the edges of the room to work out the bird instinct before it took hold. He felt better with a bit of air under his wings. Taking another circle, he landed and reviewed what was written on the page: they were his words, describing events before the Sorcerer's fire. He wrote them, but these were not in his hand. A copy.

He paced back and forth on the arm of the couch, working out how and why and ... He stopped. Brooke had the answers. Knowing her, they would be filled with care and goodness. No need to worry. Let her sleep.

His looked at the magnificent palace she made for him. "I am truly home," he tweeted, and stretched his wings, relishing the idea.

The last time he'd known such contentment was as a librarian.

Ben took to the air, gliding, knowing exactly what to do. He was home; he'd reestablish his morning routine from those peaceful days: exercise, then the perfect spot to settle in for a morning meditation.

Push, push, and up through the skylight into the blue.

"Of all the people (and birds) in all the world, what are the chances that you and I should meet?" the Princess wondered aloud, lying on a blanket, hands behind her head, looking up at the ceiling. She watched the fluffy clouds through the glass, changing shapes as they passed. They were surrounded by the remnants of a picnic lunch Brooke had arranged. The large book lay open off to the side.

Ben was cracking open a seed.

"It must be for a reason," she continued. Turning her head to see Ben, "Do you believe that? That things happen for a reason?"

"No, I don't," he said. Crack. "I think events occur, and people create reasons to make them feel as though they have a destiny or some such thing."

"Well, that's no fun," Brooke said. "Calling it a destiny makes it sound like an adventure. It's more romantic and exciting, don't you think?"

The little bird took a breath and sighed.

"Oh, I guess not."

"I don't, actually," Ben said. "I'm sorry to disappointment you."

"What? Why would you be a disappointment?" she asked.

"Because I don't agree with you."

"You are a silly bird. Who'd want to be around someone who agreed with them all the time?" she asked. "That'd be like talking to a mirror. Boring."

"I agree completely," Ben said.

Brooke laughed. Ben chirped.

"Getting your castle-legs back, huh?" she asked.

"Yes, quite," he said.

"Oh," Brooke, said, hitting the floor with her hand and making him jump. "Let's go see the library. Would you like to?" She was already up and cleaning up the picnic area.

"That would be so tweet – I mean sweet – no, neat. Uh," he said, shaking his head. "Yes, I would like to."

Brooke put away the folded blanket. "Very well, follow me," she said and headed for the door. Ben followed. "On the way, you can tell me about the fire."

That stopped Ben in midair, "What?" He started flapping.

"Ben," she said calmly. "I know you're stuck with those feathers, but you're going to have to grow a little thicker hide."

"Yes, yes," he said, taking a swoop around in a circle to feel the air. "You're right." A second circle was smoother.

"There you go," Brooke said.

"Much better," he said joining her at the door.

"I'm so proud of you," she told him, smiling. Then, "So, the fire."

Following her out the door: "Whatever happened to ... 'You don't have to tell me anything if you don't want to?'"

She stopped short and turned to Ben as he caught up with her. "You ... you don't want to tell me?"

"It's just ... It's not that," he said. "I do want to tell you, but–"

"Great," she said with a smile and headed down the stairs. "So, where'd it start?" Stopping again, "Please don't say the library." When he didn't respond right away, "Oh no, Ben, not your library."

"I'm afraid so," he told her.

Brooke's shoulders slumped, and she continued down the stairs. "No wonder you didn't want to talk about it," she said.

After a few steps, she said, "Well, go on."

"This was some weeks after my last entry in the Record Book, and a month or more before the nuptials ..."

❀ ❀ ❀ ❀ ❀ ❀ ❀

Julianna came to see me in the library. She wanted to prepare something special for her wedding. Their romance blossomed while she read to him, and she was thinking it would be nice to recite a passage at the ceremony.

"It's perfect," I told her.

"It is lovely," Brooke interjected.

She put her hand on mine, thanked me, and then asked if I could help her find something.

The year I spent teaching Julianna to read made us quite good friends. I could never refuse her anything. I was about to tell her so when the strangest thing happened. I couldn't tweet – speak. I couldn't speak. Looking around, everything was different: sharper, more distinct. It was as though, suddenly, there were more colors than the rainbow. A color for heat, another for cold. I could see everything. And I saw him, the Sorcerer. His face was gnarled, his skin gone pale, with tints of green, and his wand was aimed directly at me!

Why would he? Why green?

"Yes, why?" Brooke asked, stopping in the hall.

That's when I saw Julianna's hand was still on mine. The jealousy. But he had to know we would never ...

Suddenly Julianna was screaming. Then an explosion of light and smoke. Before I realized it, I was floating on air. I had wings. Below, the Sorcerer's wand slashing back and forth, consuming the library in flames."

"Oh no," Brooke said.

The fire. Everywhere. Julianna. Where was she? I couldn't find her in the flames. The heat was unbearable. Burning. I flew out the high window into the courtyard – the Sorcerer extending his rampage. The man's rage was devastating. We should have left him alone ... The castle aflame, he moved onto the village: people running for their lives. The farms. He must've seen me, or he was challenging the gods themselves: raising his wand to the heavens; a bolt of lightning cracked the sky, singeing my tail feather. I didn't look back. I never looked back, throughout the night.

In the morning, too tired to go on, I landed on a branch overlooking a pool of water. It was then I saw I'd been turned into this ...

❀ ❀ ❀ ❀ ❀ ❀ ❀

They were at the top of the staircase. Ben perched on the banister. Brooke offered the palm of her hand, and he stepped onto it. She softly petted his breast, and then brought him to her cheek.

He could feel the heat as his feathers rubbed against her skin. Turning her hand so she could see the back of him, she said,

"Didn't you say he singed your tail feathers?"

"I've molted since," he explained

"Oh," she said. And, quietly, "Thank you for telling me, Ben. I'm sure it wasn't easy."

"Oh, like I had a choice," he said. "I guess we know who the Princess is around here."

Brooke's mouth dropped open.

"I'm not saying you're spoiled, exactly ..." he said, taking off down the stairs.

"I am not spoiled," she corrected him, following.

"No, no. There must be some other word to describe one who's accustomed to always getting their way," he said. "'Though I can't think of one at the moment ..."

"I'm not," she protested.

"Pampered? Indulged? No," he said fluttering at the bottom of the stairs. "I'm quite stumped."

She stopped on the bottom stair, right at Ben's eye level.

"You read quite a bit, Princess; can you think of a fitting synonym?" he asked her.

Brooke put her hands on her hips to make the point, "I am neither pampered nor indulged, and I'm definitely not spoiled," she told him.

"Of course not, Your Highness," he said. "My apologies. And that's definitely not the stance a spoiled child would adopt."

The Princess noticed how she was posed and had to bite her lips to keep from smiling. Taking her hands from her hips to show the way, "To your left is the royal library, Prince Benjamin."

"After you, Princess," he said.

At the end of a long corridor, Brooke pushed open two leather-upholstered doors, revealing the royal library: circular, two stories tall, with a balcony halfway up and several rolling ladders throughout to make every volume easily accessible. Sunlight streamed in through dozens of stained glass windows, bathing the room in a spectrum of colors.

The Prince fluttered around the room, higher and higher, suddenly bursting out in a pure Parakeet song. Everywhere he went, there were posts and perches of various sizes and material, from thin wooden dowels to actual tree branches, jutting out from shelves, bookcases, banisters, window-sills, even the ladders had a few. He landed on a long branch, close to the Princess. "It's a glorious room," he said. "You think of everything don't you?"

"What can I say?" she said, shrugging, "I like to spoil my friends."

"Ah, well played, Princess," he said.

Brooke did a little curtsy.

"I've been meaning to tell you ... I really don't mind being a Parakeet," Ben said. "Not now. Since I met you."

"Aww, Ben," she said, rubbing the back of her finger against her friend's chest. "You're quite beautiful, in fact."

"And I'm told I have a very pleasing chirp."

"Yes," said Brooke. "I'm the one who told you."

"Right," he said. "Well, we've already established you're the smart one."

She looked at him sideways, "And you still don't think we were destined to meet?"

Ben shook his head. He took in a big breath, and looking directly at the Princess, told her, "What I think, Your Highness is that it took two bloodlines formed from a millennium of good and great people coming together – and only through your mother's incredible strength and your father's sheer brilliance – to create your miraculous entrance to the world. You've had a million chances and a million reasons to give up, become bitter, angry, sad or resentful, but not you ... you find hope in the midst of despair; you choose to believe in the sun behind the clouds. You. No, I don't believe in some unseen force, fate or destiny – I believe you are the adventure and the romance and the excitement. I believe in you."

"Oh, Ben," the Princess said, touching her heart with her hand. "What did I do to deserve a friend like you?"

The Parakeet cocked his head back and forth, confused. "Why ... everything," he said.

~ *X* ~

Chimeras

spell isn't born out of thin air ... it's created by harnessing the primal forces of nature and transforming them into an unnatural power.

No one can say for sure what connections an enchantment might put in motion – not even the conjurer. It's not by chance that a Prince is drawn to the very forest where only he can break a spell; a Princess discovers the secret entrance to a room where she is destined to prick her finger, or a young boy makes the worst bargain ever for the sale of his cow and ends up with a few magic beans. Myths, fairy tales, and fables are full of happenstance and coincidences that are actually the unseen threads of a magical incantation.

Magic with bad intent is a disruption of nature, like stopping the rain from falling. Sooner or later, life will find a way, and the rains will come – you can run from it or you can weather the storm, knowing that with the sun's love, new life will come.

❀ ❀ ❀ ❀ ❀ ❀ ❀

The dreams began with the first crimson moon, returning each month, in tune with its cycle. With her room being so close to the celestial body, they fell subject to its pull, like the tides: growing in intensity as the circle fully bloomed.

Brooke hadn't experienced any visions since her flight with Ben through the enchanted forest. At first, it was hard to tell what they were about. Like most dreams, they vanished in the early morning haze of waking. This morning was different.

This morning, she awoke with an overwhelming feeling of freedom like she'd never known …

Ben was in his cage. He pulled his beak out from under his wing and shook his tiny head. He heard the Princess before he saw her, breathing deeply, on the edge of crying. She was holding her breast with both of her delicate hands, as though she was going to faint – maybe she was.

"What it is, Your Highness? Are you alright?" he asked, taking flight, fluttering over her head as she jumped from the bed and paced around the room, trying to catch her breath.

"It's so beautiful," she said. "And so sad."

She walked around in circles until she finally fell back on her bed. After a time, her breath returned to normal. "My goodness. Oh, my goodness. I had no idea you could fly so high," she told her friend who'd settled on the footboard.

"I'm not sure what you mean?" he said.

She lifted an arm up toward the glass ceiling and the purple-gray clouds of pre-dawn. "I felt as if we could touch the heavens."

Ben cocked his head back and forth, "We?" he said, "I wasn't flying last night."

"Hmm," Brooke said, sitting up, searching the skies for the answers. Then it struck her: "Maybe I'm sharing your dreams. Is that what you dream about?" she asked.

"Now, that's a subject of much debate: whether or not budgies dream. Some talk or squawk in the night, much like a dog runs as though chasing a carriage. Being a human in parakeet form ..."

Brooke let out a half sigh/half grunt.

"Right," he said, getting it. "The few dreams I can recall were of me walking again."

"Oh. Oh yes, of course. Sorry," she said.

"Perfectly alright."

"How could I know what it feels like?" she asked herself, more than him.

"Well, it was a dream," he pointed out. "The wisest men in all the world can't say for sure what's possible when a dream takes hold."

❀ ❀ ❀ ❀ ❀ ❀ ❀

As the months passed, the visions came more into focus, and yet more confusing. Always culminating in a night of beauty, terror, and everything in between when the moon was full.

Everything was black. She was somewhere. She was moving. Walking on a hard, uneven surface, slanting down: cooler air behind her, warmer in front. Her eyes adjusted to the dark. Or was it the dim light far ahead, down the winding tunnel?

It was a cave. Black as coal. The flat edges of jagged rocks reflecting the growing orange ember ahead. Following the twisting path deeper into the earth's core. Heat filling her lungs. Too hot. No more.

She couldn't turn around. Down. She could hear the flames charging up through the tunnel just beyond the next turn. Filling the cave with bright orange. The heat wrapping around her skin.

There it was below: a river of molten liquid. Bubbling up. Bursting forth a torrent of fire directly at her. Burning her.

Brooke woke up screaming in pain. Writhing in her bed.

Ben was right there with her. They had a perch built on the nightstand so he could be close on the bad nights. "It's alright. It's alright, Brooke," he said.

Queen Jessica took hold of Brooke's wrists to keep her from smacking herself, trying to put out the flames on her body. "Come home, baby," she reassured her. The Queen or King had taken to sleeping on the daybed some nights.

The nursemaid would take the couch. She handed Queen Jessica cool cloths for the Princess, who was beginning to breathe regularly again.

"That's it," Ben said, soothingly. "Welcome home, Princess."

Brooke smiled in her sleep, twisting into a stretch.

Queen Jessica was lightly wiping the curls back from her daughter's face when she froze. "Could you hand me the lamp?" she asked the nurse.

Taking the lamp, the Queen brought it close to Brooke's face.

She gasped, covered her mouth, jumping off the bed. The nurse grabbed the lamp before it dropped from Queen Jessica's hand.

"What is it, miss?" she asked the Queen, following her, helping her into the armchair.

Ben took to the air. No thoughts of flying away.

He'd seen it.

The hair around Brooke's face was singed. Burnt.

❀ ❀ ❀ ❀ ❀ ❀ ❀

How did she get back in the evil forest? Oh no.

Wait.

She could hear the night creatures around her: the screams and strangulations of monsters meeting their ends in the shadows.

There was a fire. Way down below. Through the sleepy-slits of her eyelids, she could see parts of a wide circle of fires. Was she up in the trees? It didn't feel like it. She felt heavy. Grounded.

Her back was against a pole or something. She wasn't a bird; that's for sure. Why couldn't she keep her eyes open? So sleepy. She itched, on her arm. Scratched it. Sounded like sandpaper. Felt like rawhide.

It was a bug or something, biting her. Stinging. She squished it between thick fingers. Crunching, too, like brittle twigs. Muffled cries.

"Oh, my goodness. Did I just snore? Gross."

Her mouth was wide open. Wait, now what? Something pulled at her jaw. The bottom. Her teeth? Was something in her teeth? She tried to shake it off. She didn't want to wake up.

Darn it. It was tugging now. Definitely in her teeth. Winding around the lower row. Something twisting, thick on her tongue now. Growing fatter and fatter and down her throat. Choking.

"Okay, I guess I have to wake up a little, after all. What's that?"

Some thick, snaky vine filling up her mouth, heading down her pipes toward her stomach.

"Alright. If that's how you want to play."

She bit down on it. Liquid spewed out either end. She wiped the retreating leftover vine juice off her chin and used the milky slime in her mouth to help her chew the rest of the vine. She helped it down to her stomach with a big swallow.

"Now can I sleep?"

❀ ❀ ❀ ❀ ❀ ❀ ❀

She opened her eyes to see her father's strong face. Her smile was automatic.

"That wasn't such a bad night," he told her.

"Um-mm," she said shaking her head.

Getting up, "How about some breakfast? You hungry?" he asked her.

She felt her tummy. Surprised, she gave another, "Um-mm," shaking her head.

He headed for the door. "Join us for some tea when you're ready," he suggested.

Brooke nodded, but he was already out the door.

The nurse followed him out.

"Hey," Ben chirped from his nightstand stoop.

Another automatic smile, seeing him.

"What's going on?" he asked her.

She looked around, not sure what he meant.

"Why aren't you talking?"

She opened her mouth to say, "I can talk," but as soon as her mouth opened, she went into spasms. She choked and grabbed at her mouth with her fingers.

"Up, up! Out of bed, now!" he yelled at her.

She rolled out of bed onto the floor, choking and holding her throat, gasping for air.

"Stand up," he demanded.

Her face was turning purple, her body jerking back and forth.

"Brooke, you have to stand up!" he screamed.

She planted one foot.

"Push!"

She pushed her knee with both hands and got the other foot on the floor. She rose as far as she could, still bent over, her face turning blue.

She looked up to see Ben flying, full speed, right at her face. She lost her balance and fell backward. Smack. On her back.

In one huge cough, the end of a thick vine shot out of her mouth.

Ben grabbed it with his talons and pulled.

Brooke took hold of the vine and yanked it out, hand over hand until the last tendrils cleared her throat.

Air. She could breathe again. She rolled to her side, alternating between coughing and deep breathing. Her color came back.

"Oh, my goodness," she said. Her arms were wobbly, pushing herself off the floor.

That's when she saw Ben whipping the vine around with his talons, stabbing it with his hard beak.

The thing was still alive!

Coiling like a snake, it struck, wrapping itself around Ben's legs.

Ben took flight. The vine lost its grip, freeing one of the bird's legs.

"Ben, no," Brooke screamed, as he made a bee-line for the flames of the open fireplace.

The vine was rising, ready to strike again. Ben pulled up short, inches from the burning logs. The momentum sent the evil thing into the fire. Screaming and spraying white liquid. Sizzling.

Ben fluttered too close to the flames for safety until the last strings of the thing wrapped around his foot were consumed by the heat. The tip of his wing caught fire, and he fell.

Brooke's cupped hands were there to catch him inches from the fire. She rushed him to his cage, dipped her nightgown in his birdbath and gently cooled his wing. His legs were burned black.

Tears flowed from her eyes. She shook them out of the way and kept working on her friend's injuries.

❀ ❀ ❀ ❀ ❀ ❀ ❀

Each stroke of her powerful wings launched her miles ahead in the blue-black sky. The mountains below gave way to rolling hills, pastures, outcroppings of farms, a village, another, then another, growing closer and closer together until the sprawl and flickering lights of the city lay out before her. There, on the hill, outlined by its high, stone walls, the castle loomed – its delicate spires poking the clouds.

She came to roost on the highest steeple.

❀ ❀ ❀ ❀ ❀ ❀ ❀

Rising from her bed. The glass sky above clouded in mist. Fog pouring in through the open skylight, shrouding the sapling, rolling across the floor, creeping into every corner.

Was it a fog?

No.

It smelled of ... smoke.

Wait. Something's wrong. Was she dreaming?

Brooke turned and stared back at the bed. Was that her, asleep beneath the covers? No. A rumpled mess of pillows and blankets? Was it? The mix of light and shadow made it impossible to tell.

Brooke grabbed a chair and headed toward the opening in the roof. Knee-deep in the floating mist, standing on the seat, propped up against the planter, she leaned forward, pulled the leafy branches apart and shooed away the thick smoke to get a view skyward.

A thick, black-red, scaly tail of some unknown beast thumped down on top of the roof. Dragging, screeching across the glass, it swept the fog aside.

Leaning forward to peer through the opening in the mist,

Brooke tipped forward and disappeared.

A strong gust of wind blew through the opening as the Princess reappeared. The fog scattered. Looking up, another gust blasted through the opening. Brooke shielded her face against the swirling debris it kicked up from the planter.

When she lowered her hands, the night sky was clear, the full moon, shining bright and the room quiet, but for the gentle rustling of leaves.

"Did you see that? Did you see it?" Brooke asked, turning to Ben's empty cage. The nightstand perch was bare.

"What was it, dear?" her mother said, rising from the daybed.

"Your Highness," the nursemaid said, coming to her from the couch.

"Where's Ben," the Princess asked.

"In the library, I believe, miss," the nurse said. "Where he is most nights."

"What is it, dearest?" the Queen asked putting on her robe. "What happened? Are you alright?"

"I'm fine," she told her. "Really. I just need to see Ben. You go back to sleep."

The nursemaid had already grabbed Brooke's robe and slippers. Brooke thanked her.

"Are you sure?" Queen Jessica asked.

Brooke had her robe on. "I'm sure," she said, slipping into her shoes. "Get some sleep."

The library doors banged open, sending papers and Ben flying.

Brooke rushed to the massive oak table. Pushing everything off, she threw down a sheet of parchment, grabbed pieces of charcoal and started drawing.

"Are you alright?" Ben asked, landing on his favorite branch, overlooking the table.

"I wish everyone would stop asking me that," she muttered under her breath. Furiously drawing.

"So, now I'm everyone," he said. "I suppose that's better than being, 'they'."

Brooke stopped for a second and smiled at her friend.

"Good morning, Your Highness," he said, bowing.

"Good morning to you, Your Highness," she said, bowing back, and then returned to her drawing.

Ben looked at it with each eye, and then flew up to a second-floor perch to get more perspective. "It's the castle ... How ...?"

Still drawing, she glanced up at her friend. "This is what it looks like, doesn't it? From above?"

Ben nodded.

"Who was I?" she asked the drawing. "What was I?"

Ben watched his friend put her hands on the table, straight-armed, her shoulders shaking. He couldn't tell if she was laughing or crying. Droplets hit the charcoal lines, smearing edges of the castle. Ben floated down to the table.

She lifted her head. Apparently, she was doing both. Barely containing her laughter, with tears streaming down her face, Brooke said, "I don't know what's going on, but I'm outside all the time in my dreams." She leaned closer to him. "This spell is coming apart at the seams. Let's rip it open some more."

"We don't know what that might do," he said. "You could be lost in a nightmare."

"I may be by the next full moon if nothing changes," she told him.

"We don't even know how," he argued.

"I'm sure you'll think of something," she said, rubbing his breast with her fingertip. "After all, you're the smart one."

"No, that's you, Brooke."

"Oh. Really?" she asked. "That doesn't sound right."

Ben took her hand in his (well, he wrapped his three toes around one finger). Both of his little legs were still scarred and black. "I'll think of something," he assured her.

She smiled and gave him a little peck on his golden feathers. "Look at it this way," she said, standing upright, "For better or worse ... You'll be making my dream come true."

~ *XI* ~

The Winds Of Change

Not every month was bad. Those that were, were dangerously so.

Something had to be done. These were the people to do it.

You know how different people in different places come up with the same idea at the same time?

"I was just thinking the same thing."

There's a reason you hear that so often. Ideas are in the air. If you're watching or listening, you can hear them blowin' in the wind.

If you're a person who's used to making things happen, you act.

❀ ❀ ❀ ❀ ❀ ❀ ❀

As a rule, parakeets sleep from dusk till dawn. Ben had stuck to that pattern, mostly.

Not anymore – not since the evil vine crossed a bridge that shouldn't exist: the one between the dream world and reality.

Not right away, either. His claws had been so badly burnt. He couldn't stand up for weeks. Or perch.

Sleeping. You don't know what it's like not to be able to roost. Try setting your bed at a forty-five-degree angle. It's like that. Very disconcerting.

He'd never tell Brooke, or the King and Queen, but he was in pain every day.

He spent much of his days fluttering around the library, searching for books that might offer him the key to break the spell (or rip it open, as Brooke would say). At night, the library doors were propped open enough for him to fly through. A lamp kept burning. Books he'd selected were laid out on the oak table, with a dish of honey nearby. (Brooke came up with this: Ben could dip his claw into honey, making it sticky enough to turn the pages.)

For months, he'd been pouring over volumes of dusty histories, manuscripts on alchemy, psychics, herbology, philosophy, and astronomy – searching for clues. He was sure the answer was there, somewhere.

Locked away in a dark room of his little birdy brain, in the bottom drawer under a stack of borrowed books, a thought nudged away at him. He'd read something ...

What was it?

❀ ❀ ❀ ❀ ❀ ❀ ❀

She could hear it from down the hall. Metal against metal. What were they doing in there?

The maid who came to her room said, "The King wishes to

see you in the great hall, miss."

Brooke asked what for.

"It's not for me to say, miss," was her response. "He did mention that you should be comfortably dressed and wear practical shoes."

Practical? What does that mean? To save the servant from explaining, "It's not for her to say," again; Brooke thanked her and told her to tell the King she'd be down presently.

Practical.

They only used the great hall for, well, great stuff.

There were bits of straw strewn about the entrance to the hall. Up ahead, the floor was covered in it.

Rounding the corner, she saw her father sword-fighting with a thin, gray-haired gentleman. He was really old: at least forty, maybe even forty-five, yet kind of ... dashing. The two men were pretty evenly matched, but the old man was very calm about the whole thing while her father was struggling and sweating.

Other, much younger men were engaged in swordplay, some using wooden weapons. There was an array of weaponry along the wall: bows and arrows, spears, staffs, targets down at the far end, straw dummies standing at attention with poles up their backs.

One of the young men caught sight of Brooke and bowed, "Your Highness."

Everyone stopped what they were doing and bowed.

Except, of course, the King. "Hello Princess," he said, catching his breath. He handed his sword and glove to a waiting squire. "You arrived just in time to save Lord Hester from an embarrassing defeat."

"I'm in your debt, Princess," the Lord said with a bow.

"Great," she said, "I'll try to come up with a way for you to repay me."

Lord Hester looked confused.

The King patted him on the shoulder, "You might want to watch what you say."

Brooke followed her dad to a buffet table loaded with fruits, meats, and cheeses. "Remember what I used to tell you when you were little, and you had a bad dream?" he asked her.

"Umm. Go back to sleep?"

"No," he said. "Maybe sometimes." He handed her a plate, piled high. "Here, eat."

"I'm not really hungry," she told him.

He looked at her.

She started eating.

"You're going to need your strength," he told her, making a plate for himself. "I'd tell you: they're your dreams; you're in control. If you're scared or need help, you can bring me in. I'll protect you."

"Oh yeah," she said.

They sat down at a small table.

"I'm not sure if that'll work in your current situation, but your mother's bringing in some people who might be able to help there."

"Who?"

"I don't know," he told her. "She's met a lot people who aren't necessarily considered 'castle-friendly'."

Brooke nodded.

"I thought it'd be a good idea for you to learn how to protect yourself," he said. "Just in case."

"'Sounds practical," she said, looking at her shoes.

"Couldn't hurt," he said. "From what you've said, you have an active part in these visions."

Brooke nodded.

Her father was very straightforward, logical in his thinking. Calm exterior. It was only the wringing of his hands that gave away how deeply concerned he was for his little girl. (Well, young woman now; she was fifteen.)

Brooke placed her too-thin hand on her father's. Bringing them a bit of peace – as he'd done for her so many times.

"Not the typical Princess education," he said. "But since when has this family ever been considered typical."

❀ ❀ ❀ ❀ ❀ ❀ ❀

Her training began the very same hour

Like Ben, combat wasn't very high on her list of things to do. She never saw the art in war. To her, the 'sweet science' of boxing was neither. Archery appealed to her, slightly – only because she looked up the word for an archer, and it gave her chance to say to Ben, "I'm a bit of a toxophilite."

"Haha," he chirped, "I love the way you talk."

Brooke felt very much the way she described her mother when she took off into the unknown with Beau: Everything she'd ever learned being a Princess was no good to her at all.

Everything she assumed: wrong. Every romantic notion: shattered. Every logical conclusion: not even close.

The training? Ugh. It was nothing like what she'd read in myths and legends. The unnecessarily cruel, Lord 'Fester,' – which was what she called him (only when talking to Ben) – had her doing this crab-crawling stance for weeks, developing the muscles in her legs before he even let her handle a sword – a wooden one.

All the other young men she assumed were there for her to spar with? They weren't.

Her father had purchased Lord Hester's school, and these were squires and knights in training.

Any romantic tale would have had these lads secretly adore the brave, warrior Princess. Nope. They resented her for stealing their master's attention from their own training.

She never felt more like a 'Princess.'

❀ ❀ ❀ ❀ ❀ ❀ ❀

So, the people (if you could call them that) that her mother brought in ... Whoa.

Again, not all like it was in stories: floating fairies, friendly godmothers, fatherly figures spouting wisdom. Uh-uh. Dirty, smelly, crazy folk. They were living on the outskirts of town because they belonged on the outskirts of life.

It was strange. They were strange. (But here's the thing: stuff that seems weird now, might make perfect sense later. 'Specially when you're a teenager. I know. I used to be one, and

I've parented a few. You don't fit in at school. Nobody likes you. Your parents tell you to join a club or start one of your own. That's stupid: only weirdos and nerds join clubs. Day after day they tell you, week after week. Two semesters later, you explain how you came up with this great idea to start a club, and ten students have already signed up. It's the motivated students who want to get ahead that join clubs.)

The first was supposed to be a wood nymph, except she was really old, ratty-haired, and had painted on lips. Brooke wondered if her fingernails were made of wood. They looked like the bark of a tree: long, brown, and cracked. She waved them about as she spoke.

Next was a pair of witches. One had only a right eye – the other, only a left. When they put their heads together, the eyes worked together. Brooke was dying to know what would happen if they switched places. Would they be cross-eyed?

It didn't matter if the visitor was clearly out of their mind, they were always treated as an honored guest: fed and paid for their services. Brooke and Queen Jessica were never discouraged.

Not that you could see, anyway.

❀ ❀ ❀ ❀ ❀ ❀ ❀

Funny, of all the uses for your hands, it was times like this where Ben missed them the most. Slamming this book closed to mark that 'aha,' moment would be so gratifying. He didn't remember the solution he was searching for – he remembered the most important thing he'd learned from a lifetime of study: most answers aren't found on the pages of books.

He took flight.

Floating down the hallway, he imagined his father's hand on his shoulder. He was, what, eleven at the time? The King had found him that morning, sitting on the floor of the library, surrounded by stacks of books, bleary-eyed and teary-eyed. He'd spent the entire night searching for a solution to a problem his philosophy teacher had given him.

His eleven-year-old self had no idea what his father was talking about. Of course, the answers are in the books, that's what books are for. His father told him, "No, my son. Books are written to stimulate this," tapping Benjamin's forehead, "... and inspire this," he explained, putting his large hand over Ben's heart.

The young Prince was even more confused.

His father pointed to the door at the end of the corridor. "Let's say, behind that door is the answer to your problem. You read every book you can find on how to fashion keys: on lock picking, on how doors are constructed and hung. Nothing works," he tells him. "But look, here's a window, and it's a beautiful day, so you go outside instead – leaving the problem behind."

"How does that help?" young Ben asked.

"I don't know," the King told him. "Maybe from outside you can see a window open on the other side of the door. Maybe watching the clouds, you wonder how the room beyond the door circulates air, and you find a chimney flue to gain access. Maybe you forget about the door, and that night as you pass, you see light flickering beneath the door, so you simply knock and someone inside opens it."

"Obtaining knowledge isn't the goal," his father explained, "it's what you do with it that counts."

Prince Benjamin Parakeet banked left and flew out the window into the morning air.

There's something about the open sky; up high, halfway to the clouds, where the air is thin and pure. Its untainted power opens your lungs, clearing the cobwebs from your mind.

Ben wasn't searching for answers in the clouds. Clouds don't hold answers, silly birds – only the distant parade of your imagination.

He came to roost on the washroom window. (It was left open, even in winter, allowing the steam from the boiling water to escape.) The moist air flowed through his feathers. There he settled into his daily meditation. He'd practiced this Eastern technique since discovering the writings of the Pali Canon in the Sorcerer's library.

The solution to how he could help his best friend didn't come to him as most ideas do – with a spark of inspiration and days of weighing its merits. By the time he'd settled atop Brooke's dressing table mirror an hour later, the plan was fully formulated.

"Good morning, Ben," the Princess said with a smile.

He could tell it still took some effort for Brooke to keep up her familiar cheerfulness: the circles under her eyes were fading as her body grew stronger from over a year of daily training. Her hair was tied up with a purple ribbon all the time – it was darker now and had lost a bit of luster.

The sparkle in her eyes was a constant.

"Brooke," he said.

She jumped a bit, having already forgotten he was there. Then she frowned, realizing that he had called her by name – which he almost never did: 'Princess,' mostly, 'my friend,' in quieter times, and, 'your highness,' when he was being formal or lapsing into his 'Librarian/Teacher' mode.

"What's wrong?" she asked him.

"Not a thing," he assured her. Then after a moment, "I know of a way for you to go outside."

She bit her lower lip. "Oh, Ben," is all she could say.

"Before I explain," he said, "you have to keep in mind that even if it works, you won't actually be able live in the outdoors or enjoy it very much, but you may be able to walk or ride – no flying, for sure."

Brooke smiled.

"Would that be of use to you?" he asked.

"Oh yes," she told him. "I know how to appreciate a gift of any size."

"I've never done it, nor seen it done, and we'll have to depend on my memory of a document I read years ago," he explained.

"I understand," she said, smiling. She found him so adorable when he got all serious and protective.

Brooke motioned with her head, asking him to join her. She rested her cheek on top of the dressing table, and Ben fluttered down.

He leaned in with his tiny, feathered head. Rubbing his cheek against hers, he cooed.

❀ ❀ ❀ ❀ ❀ ❀ ❀

She'd never known physical pain. Now she did. Almost daily.

More than a year into her training, in the middle of a wrestling match, her opponent sent an elbow to her face (not a wrestling move, by any stretch). She heard a crack in her jaw and dropped to the straw.

She felt the young squire wrap her up in a sure pinning hold.

When she regained her focus, she saw Lord Hester's face, watching her.

In seconds that drew on like an hour, she understood his place: this man loved her. Not like, 'love,' love.

A warrior kind of love: Honor.

He'd accepted the honor of saving her life. In the real world or the dream one. That was his purpose. His quest.

His honor was tied to her success.

His face showed no guilt from the pain she was in or worry that she might fail. He was ... hopeful.

Yes. He believed in her, but why? What did he know about her to justify that faith? She was getting beat up and worn down every day. What kind of idiot keeps coming back for more abuse?

"Oh," she thought, "one who wants to succeed. Someone who can take it and keep trying."

People may tell you: "Never bend to the will of others." They see a line in the sand that can't be crossed. I'm not saying they're wrong. (Idiots are placed in our path to clearly mark a 'dip' in the road.) What I can tell you is this: the Princess showed more strength than most who appear strong because she said, "I will bend, but I will not break."

She stopped fighting against the wrestling squire. With no effort at all, she slid free. She watched her hand twist the young soldier's head to the side, driving his face into the straw, pinning him.

Lord Hester motioned with his finger for her to come.

Finally, now she would get some recognition for all of her hard work. Instead, he placed his hands on either side of her jaw, feeling where it was dislocated, and then suddenly jammed it back into place with a crack.

"Again," he said, with only the smallest nod to Princess Brooke.

The first step to understanding her power came from knowing herself.

❀ ❀ ❀ ❀ ❀ ❀ ❀

One afternoon, a guard found an old gentleman outside the castle gate. He appeared lost. The man had the same unruly look of some of the Queen's recent visitors and was brought before Brooke and Queen Jessica.

"This fellow claims to be a Seer," the guard told them, "yet couldn't find his way through the castle gate," he added.

The man was really, really old. Way older than Lord Hester. As old as dust. No kidding, whenever he moved his arms, dust would fly.

He listened intently as Brooke explained some of her dreams

in detail. Saying, "Yes, yes," as though he understood. When she described the Sorcerer's green complexion, he sat up in his chair.

"Have you been put under a spell, perchance?" he asked. "Not a curse, but a spell."

"Why, yes," Brooke said.

"You," he said, pointing his old, old finger at her. "Not you?" he asked, pointing it at Queen Jessica.

"That's right," the Queen told him.

"May I?" he asked, holding out his old, old hand to take Brooke's. She placed her hand in his wrinkly one.

"Hmm," he said, closing his eyes. He opened them after a few seconds. "I have nothing to tell you that you don't already know."

"Ugh, is this one of those riddles?" Brooke asked. "I hate those."

"Brooke," her mother scolded.

Brooke's hand covered her mouth, "That was rude. Please forgive me."

The old, old man was laughing. "I hate them, too," he said. "I can't believe that came out of my mouth." His laugh became a wheeze. For a moment, it seemed like he ran out of breath and might die right there.

He didn't. Thank goodness.

A servant brought the old, old man some water, and he thanked them. "These dreams, Princess," he said, "... are not your own?"

Brooke shook her head.

"No?" he asked, squinting at her. "What would yours be?"

The Queen looked at her daughter while she considered the question.

"Well, they are outside," Brooke said. "So, I guess, in that way, they're like my own."

"Ah," he said, nodding. "Perhaps, you share them?"

"Maybe," she said.

The old, old man grunted his approval. He pushed himself up from the chair.

The Princess stood up with him. "Do you think I could make them more my own?" she asked him.

He shrugged, heading for the door. "Anything's possible," he said.

Brooke's mouth dropped open. She looked at her mom, who raised her eyebrows. "Wait," she said to the old, old man, "how would I ..." But he was gone.

Brooke ran out to the door. He was nowhere to be seen. She asked the guard and the servant waiting in the hallway, "Where did he go?"

"Your Highness?" the guard asked, unsure of what she was asking.

The servant shook her head, confused as well.

Brooke looked around.

He was gone.

After a moment, she smiled.

Then laughed out loud.

~ *XII* ~

Outside

"There are several ways you can improve your brain," Ben explained. .

"Ooo. What are they?" Brooke asked. She bounced in her chair at the big oak table in the library.

Ben paced along the branch above her – the stain glass sunlight bathing him in orange and purples. "Meditation being one."

"What are the others?"

"Oh, ah … various things: exercise–"

"I do a lot of that now," she said.

"Reading, sleeping–"

"Oh, I'm gonna be brilliant," she said.

"Without a doubt," he assured her. "Meditation helps to shrink the part of your brain that controls fears and anxieties–"

"Perfect for your birdy side," she said.

"And has helped me enormously," he told her. "It's known to

expand the part of your brain that exudes happiness."

"Yay," Brooke said.

He explained how he'd discovered papers in the Sorcerer's library regarding a relaxation technique called, 'Transcendental Meditation'. "Although I haven't found it to be very transcending, myself. Some consider it the opposite of true meditation."

She gave him a look.

"But I digress," he said. "It's an exercise for your mind. You concentrate on your breathing in an effort to free your mind of thoughts, feelings, emotions, and desires. By letting go of what is, basically, yourself, you find peace."

"Oh, I like that."

"I believe that if you can truly achieve this state of bliss, you could remain 'inside' your mind, even when you're outdoors," he explained.

"Outside," she said to herself.

"To get outside, you'll have to walk while you're in a state of deep meditation. Not a common practice," he said, looking to her, in case she might be worried. Instead, she was practically giddy with excitement. "But, as we know, you're not what one would consider common."

"Smart bird."

"In addition, we're dealing with the inner workings of magic – which can be unpredictable. Is the power of an incantation in the words? Can we 'trick' a spell?"

"I like that you called it a spell," she said.

"Well, it's certainly not a curse, is it?" Ben said.

"It certainly isn't," the Princess said. "I'm just curious ..."

"Yes?" Ben asked, prepared to defend his hypothesis.

"When you were human, did people hug you all the time?" she asked him. "Girls in particular?"

"Ah ... No, actually."

"Hmm. Well, I certainly will when you're you again," she told him.

"When I'm ...?" Nothing had ruffled his feathers in quite a while. This did. "When I'm human, do you mean?"

"Yes, of course," she told him, matter-of-factly. "Why do you think we're doing this?"

"Well, I thought ..." he shook his feathers out. "I suppose I didn't think."

"That doesn't sound like you," she said.

"No, it doesn't," he said. "I don't believe I'm the same me I've always been."

Brooke laughed. "No."

"No, indeed," he said, chirping. "You've had a profound effect on me, Princess."

"You mean, you're crazy about me," she said.

"What?" he said. "I didn't ... I said nothing of the sort."

"Tomatoes, potatoes," she said, waving it away.

"That doesn't even make sense," he said.

"Mmmhmm," Brooke said, resting her elbow on the table and her cheek in her hand, staring at him.

"You're infuriating," he told her, stomping his little birdy feet on the branch.

"I know; I'm terrible," she said. "Maybe you should get back to experimenting on me. See if you can make some improvements."

"What?"

"You know. Creating this blissful life for me," she said. "Making my dreams come true."

"I never said that ... exactly."

"Didn't you? Oh," she said. "I must've misunderstood your intentions ... professor."

"Did I?"

Brooke shrugged, smiling at him.

❧ ❧ ❧ ❧ ❧ ❧ ❧

Do you know what it's like to start off on an adventure and see the road up ahead, the railroad tracks laid out before you, the trail, the river, the open sea; that catch in your breath, the beat of your heart as you start off down an uncharted path?

Brooke had never felt that thrill before. Unfortunately, excitement is kind of the opposite of what meditation is about.

She couldn't help it. She wanted to be outside. She wanted to break free.

After the old, old man's visit, Brooke was no longer tossing and turning or waking up in the middle of the night. Over time, as the moon completed its circle and its cycle, Ben could be found roosting in his cage again, her parents and nursemaid back in their rooms.

Everyone assumed the worst was over.

It was ... the worst of it.

Try as she might, she couldn't bring her father into her

visions, but the Princess was learning to control them.

When she flew, she would steer the beast that shared her consciousness toward the enchanted forest – pulling up short every time.

Surely they could defeat the mutilated devils populating the space above the canopy? Why not go after the Sorcerer in his lair?

One night, she managed to force her dream-sharing partner over the evil forest. Her wings shriveled instantly, and she nose-dived toward the dark growth. Banking hard right with what was left of her steering power, she crashed into the treetops at the edge of the wood. Grotesque night creatures screeched and dug their claws into her as she toppled toward the mound of bleached bones at the forest edge.

The dying screams of the monsters filled her ears as their hides disintegrated.

Brittle skeletons ripped her flesh as she crashed into the pile. Tumbling forward, she planted her feet hard onto the sure ground and shook her massive self, flinging bits of shattered bone into the air.

She bent her head toward the sky and filled the night with her scream.

The cry felt like fire in her throat.

Fire.

When Brooke dreamt of being in the evil forest, it was always through some large creature, and not the same one: close, but not exactly. The monsters appeared as baby beasts to her – she swatted and squished them if they dared to attack.

She sensed someone or something with her – another presence – but she was too groggy to explore further.

And fire: little bonfires on the ground, all around – the only light, so she felt, more than saw things. Whenever she forced her sleepy self to venture beyond the fires, into the darkness, vines would wrap around her thick fingers, monsters would bite, plants would spit needles, gases or stinging goo. Fire seemed to discourage the growth and the monsters.

Fire.

In the dark tunnel leading to the river of lava, she now felt comforted by the pulsing waves of scorching heat. They were her friends.

Fire was a part of her.

Awake, Brooke could place her hand over the flame of a candle. Watch her skin blister and blacken, hear it crackle. No pain. The black would fade, as it had after being scorched from words in the records of Athenaeum.

She knew she was pushing into the edges of a nightmare.

In more ways than one, she was moving too close to the fire.

❈ ❈ ❈ ❈ ❈ ❈ ❈

Day after day, Lord Hester repeated it, "You're trying too hard, Princess."

How can you try too hard? Isn't that the whole idea of trying?

The way he said it, got her back up. "You're trying too hard … Princess." All of these young men in training, yet she was the only one called out. The girl – the spoiled Princess – wasn't doing it right.

If he said it one more time, she was going to snap.

She waited for it. She shot off arrow after arrow, each landing in and around the bulls-eye. Another quiver, another five steps back: excellent shots, every one. Not perfect, though. It wasn't going to be good enough, was it? Any minute now he'd say it.

"You're trying too hard, Princess."

Ah. There it was.

She dropped the bow. "Fine," she said. She tossed the quiver, spreading the arrows out in the hay. "Then I quit."

"Precisely what you should do, Your Highness," Lord Hester said, smiling.

Brooke was having a terrible time ripping the tight archery gloves from her hands. "Oh, you'd like that wouldn't you, my Lord?"

"Very much," he told her.

"You want to see me fail," she yelled at him, fighting hard to keep the tears from spilling and her throat from catching.

"No, Your Highness," he explained. "Not fail."

She shook her head, not understanding.

The Lord came to her, offering to help with the gloves that refused to come off. Brooke put one hand in his, and he gently removed it. "Failure isn't in your vocabulary," he told her. "Neither is letting go, unfortunately. You've worked hard.

Harder than many of the young men in this room ..."

Brooke looked around. Most of the men grudgingly agreed.

"Trust it," he told her, removing the glove from her other hand. "Take a break. Let it go. Have a drink, for heaven's sake," he said. "You're old enough. You've earned it."

She was. She did. Why hadn't she thought of it before?

"I'm buying," one of the squires yelled out. Three or four others offered to do the same.

"What do you say, Brooke?" Lord Hester asked her.

She almost smiled. "Yeah," she said, "Alright."

The room erupted in laughter.

Now she smiled.

"I'll have tea, though."

Groans from the men.

"With a teaspoon of brandy," she added.

Cheers.

"Fair enough," Lord Hester said.

"But I'm buying," she said. "It's not that I don't trust you. I don't, at all, by the way – I've seen you fight. I just happen to know where the King stores the best wine."

More laughter and cheers.

"If you're going to drink with a Princess," she added, "you may as well get used to the good stuff."

❀ ❀ ❀ ❀ ❀ ❀ ❀

After months with little success from doing too much, Brooke was treated with months of success from doing very little.

Her second lesson was ... to trust herself.

❀ ❀ ❀ ❀ ❀ ❀ ❀

That was just the beginning.

Next was learning to meditate while walking. It's almost impossible. Almost.

For Princess Brooke, if you put "almost" in front of "impossible" it meant, possible.

In time, she could move through the quiet back hallways of the castle, allowing the soft flutter of Ben's wings to lead her.

She tried hundreds of times to walk outside – hundreds.

But after that first step, she'd disappear.

Ben would swoop back inside. Her mouth and forehead scrunched up. "I think I know what I did wrong," she'd say. "Yeah." Then she'd smile. "Next time, Ben, we're going outside. I can feel it."

"Next time," he'd echo back, "I'm sure of it." He was, too. If anyone in the world could make this work out of sheer will, it was his friend, Princess Brooke.

"I believe you will, Princess," they heard the King say.

He was leaning against the wall a few feet away. Who could tell how long he'd been watching? (Knowing him, quite awhile.)

"Good morning, Ben," Ben chirped back a good morning (the King assumed it was good morning – he didn't know for sure).

"Quite an accomplishment being able to walk while meditating," said the King.

"You know about it?" Brooke asked.

Ben chirped again.

Brooke translated, "How?"

"I studied in the East for several years," he told them. He sat down next to his daughter on the stone steps near the entrance. "None of the staff could figure out what you two were up to. It makes sense, though."

"I didn't want to get your hopes up," she admitted.

The King smiled at her and tucked a stray lock of hair behind her ear as he often did. "You're probably the only person in the kingdom who doesn't know how exceptional you are." Then he took one of her strong hands in his and told her, "That you are going to walk outside these walls is a foregone conclusion, Princess. It's a done deal. You may as well accept it." He gave her a little kiss. "We'll let your mother be surprised."

"Thank you, Ben," the King said to the Parakeet Prince, perched on Brooke's shoulder. Then he got to his feet.

As he was walking away, the King stopped and turned back to the two friends. "Have you tried using a mantra?" he asked. "I understand they can be quite effective."

Ben and Brooke looked at each other.

A mantra is a word or phrase you repeat over and over. It helps regulate your breathing and harmonize your body, bringing focus.

Weeks later, Brooke was repeating her mantra, "Inside I'm out, outside I'm in." Her eyes were lightly shut as she allowed the gentle fluttering of Ben's wings to guide her steps.

The stone was softer here – perhaps a rug.

No, not a rug.

"Oh ..."

Her next breath filled her entire body with pretty needles. Tingling. Alive. The fragrance, the warmth, a tweet from her best friend, "Oh, my goodness, I'm outside!"

In a flash, it was gone. Back to the cool stone shadow.

She felt it, though. She would again, and again, and again, and again, and always.

Ben found his friend happily lost in a fit of crying laughter.

Seeing him reignited both. She alternated shaking her hands, unable to control them, and covering her mouth with them to contain the sobs.

When she was able to breathe again, she offered her hand, and Ben came to light on her strong, beautiful finger.

She rubbed her cheek next to his feathery one. "I'll never be able to thank you," she said. "Never."

"You never have to," he told her. "No harm in trying, though," he added.

She laughed. "True," she said. "Thank you."

"There, see? Not so difficult," he said. "I think you can do this, Brooke, I really do."

Which started her laughter and tears all over again.

She happily wasted her next few ventures outdoors by using that one second to lift her eyes to the clear blue sky. To go barefoot and feel the earth. To smell a flower.

Then they got to work.

They discovered it was best if she wore a hooded cape – to keep distractions at bay.

As she managed to get farther from the castle, the partners

made two very important discoveries: first, if the Princess would lose her concentration after entering another structure – say, the stable – she wouldn't disappear (apparently 'inside' meant 'inside anywhere'), and second, when the spell took effect, she would be sent back to whichever building she'd visited last. So if she were distracted after visiting the gatehouse, she'd be whisked back to the gatehouse.

They made a point of going inside every structure. Eventually, they got beyond the gates and braved the clamor of the city.

❀ ❀ ❀ ❀ ❀ ❀ ❀

Queen Jessica had gone back to sleeping in her room, sure, but she wasn't thrilled about it.

More than once, she tiptoed into Brooke's room late at night and read by firelight, alert to any interruptions in her daughter's steady breathing, softly padding past the sleeping Princess in the early morn.

It's not fair that her daughter had to be watched. "This world isn't fair," Queen Jessica thought as she closed the book in her lap. She wasn't reading anyway.

Wandering over to the window, she folded one leg under and took a seat in the bay window.

At the far end of the gardens was where she'd plant the saplings from Brooke's room when they outgrew the planter. Two little trees don't make an orchard, but it's a start.

Who was that?

Walking in the direction of the same trees, a young maiden wearing a light hooded cloak. Who would wear a …

Something about the figure caught her eye. What was it?

The Queen gasped. Not knowing how she knew, she ran from the room and down the stairs; she tore through the hall and out to the gardens; then through the hedges, slowing to a stop a few feet from the hooded girl. That's when she saw the snow-white Parakeet with golden feathers on its head, quietly fluttering a little ways beyond.

For a moment, Queen Jessica was afraid to move or say a word. Taking a deep breath, she managed to say her name. "Brooke."

The Princess looked up and saw her mother, who rushed at her and held her in her arms.

Immediately they found themselves back within the castle walls, still holding one another.

Ben took his time getting back inside, hoping to miss all of the crying that was bound to come from the women. A really long time.

When he found them, they were picking themselves off the floor and were now sharing handkerchiefs, dabbing the last of the tears away. Perfect timing.

"Ben," Queen Jessica said when she spotted him. "Oh, Benjamin."

Uh-oh, maybe he was a little too early. The dam might just burst.

"Mmm," the Queen said, reaching toward him, and then squeezing her fists. "How do you keep from kissing him all the time?" she asked her daughter.

"I know, right?" Brooke said.

"We're throwing you a feast, Prince Higginbotham," Queen Jessica told him. "Tonight."

"Splendid," he chirped.

"Put on your best—oh," the Queen said, catching herself. "We'll make it an informal event. Come as you are."

One tweet.

❀ ❀ ❀ ❀ ❀ ❀ ❀

That night, they threw a relaxed feast in honor of Prince Benjamin Mordecai Higginbotham.

Lord Hester and his men joined them.

Ben insisted on making a speech even though no one could understand a tweet he said, and Brooke had to translate every word.

Late in the evening as the festivities faded, the food and drink stopped flowing, the orchestra dwindled to a soft flute and the simple strings of a gentle mandolin, the King, Queen, the Princess, and the Parakeet Prince sat around the table with their crowns set aside and their laces and collars loosened.

"Now that you can venture outdoors, daughter," the King said, "What do you plan to do?"

Ben cocked his head in Brooke's direction.

The Queen sat up in her chair.

The Princess looked at each of them, one by one, "Funny you should ask ..." she said with a sly smile (and I hope Ben will excuse the analogy), like the cat that ate the canary.

~ *XIII* ~

Brooke's Company

P eople don't listen very well, they mostly wait for thier chance to talk.

The Princess learned how to listen very early on. She listened hard whenever her mother repeated her story. Not just because it was all about her (although, that's always nice), but for clues.

Her father loved puzzles. This was hers: how do I break this spell?

Brooke figured out the quieter she became, the more she heard. What she heard, buried deep within the adventures, was her mother's belief that Beauregard had more potential for love in him than hate.

That feeling stuck with her. Then she read about how the servant girl, Juliana, opened the Sorcerer's heart – that was proof positive.

That knowledge gave our Princess a weapon she knew how to

wield with more power than almost anyone alive: Hope.

No matter what madness Beauregard's jealousy had driven him to, his heart kept a small hope of redemption.

She could offer Beau the chance to save himself from falling into darkness forever.

❀ ❀ ❀ ❀ ❀ ❀ ❀

This was what Brooke believed. It's what she told the King and Queen – right before she told them that she was going to seek out the Sorcerer.

"What if you're wrong?" her father asked. "What if he's beyond caring?"

Ben tweeted a few times, shaking his little head. The King and Queen couldn't tell, but he was laughing.

"What's so funny?" Brooke asked.

Ben told her.

"Oh, huh. I do, too ..." she said. "... sometimes."

Ben kept shaking his head as Brooke translated: "Ben thinks ... Well, he told me; I'm not particularly famous for considering what to do in case I'm wrong."

Her parents both said, "Hmmm."

"Like, I always think I'm right or something," she said, shaking her head.

Her parents both said, "Hmmm," again.

"What?" she asked them. "Oh, my goodness. I'm so not like that," she argued.

"No, you're not," her father assured her.

The Queen looked at him sideways.

"It just so happens I did ... consider ... things," she said. "I know how to fight, but I don't know much about battles or strategy. Luckily, I know two very smart people who've told me the same, exact thing." She looked at her father and the Parakeet.

Ben and the King looked at each other.

"What would that be?" the King asked his daughter. "I talk a lot, so ..."

Everyone looked at the King.

"Alright. Maybe not a lot," he said.

"You both told me that one of the most important things to remember before going into battle is a true enemy would never attack from only one direction."

Ben and the King looked at each other and nodded.

"So, I will approach him as a friend, but treat him as an enemy," she said. "I would like to request a company of soldiers to join me. Sir Hester has volunteered to lead them. His knights-in-training have offered their services as well."

The King and Queen stared at their daughter.

The Queen spoke to Ben, "And you, Your Highness."

Prince Benjamin tweeted once and nodded to Queen Jessica.

"Do I have your permission, Your Majesties?"

The King and Queen looked at each other. They took a deep breath and let it out with a sigh of resignation, just like every parent of a teenager has done at one time or another.

"I'm afraid you have too much of your mother's rebellion to

keep you inside these castle walls," the King said.

Queen Jessica shook her head, adding, "I hope you have enough of your father's good sense to keep you safe."

❀ ❀ ❀ ❀ ❀ ❀ ❀

Who knows how legends begin? Some stories change with each telling. The tale about the Fire Witch of the Mountains spread throughout two kingdoms.

Only one person made it out of the evil forest, the story goes. A woman. Flames had consumed half her body, parts of her soul, and enough of her mind to drive her insane. She'd been spotted climbing the mountains of Athenaeum – which separated the two kingdoms – and vanished. For years, she'd gone unseen.

King Higginbotham sent scouts in search of her. They followed her trail to a cave chipped into the cliffs and found the charred bones of animals strewn about. They followed the tunnel deep into the earth – but no Witch.

On this side of the border, trappers in the mountains above the Olde Inn spread stories about wide patches of forest where the trees were burnt down to stumps – supposedly the work of the Fire Witch.

A woman, cloaked in black, had been reported speaking with the owner of the Olde Inn. A day later, the Inn was sold. The owner and his family rode off into the night with a large sack of silver coins.

An innkeeper was hired without ever meeting the mysterious new owner and given a set of instructions: he was forbidden to knock on or enter the wooden door leading to a set of rooms at the rear of the building, to bar anyone from disturbing the occupant, and to slide a tray of food and drink through the slot at the bottom of the door three times a day. In exchange, any profits from the inn were his to keep.

For the first few months, patrons complained about noises of construction coming from the rooms – in the years since, nothing but silence.

If the woman were the Fire Witch of the Mountains, she would be their best hope of finding their way through the evil forest.

The Olde Inn near the border of Athenaeum was to be their first stop.

❀ ❀ ❀ ❀ ❀ ❀ ❀

The best part of preparing for the journey was the time Princess Brooke spent in the royal stable.

She was given the most beautiful horse in all of the kingdom. The moment they met, everyone knew they'd be great friends. A formidable, white stallion – Brooke's height and half again – yet with a touch of her hand, the mount would kneel before her.

The royal stable was a massive structure, giving the Princess plenty of room. At first, she rode with all her senses alert; the sound of irregular-regular hooves beating on the softened floor, the feel of his flowing mane in her grip. She learned to move along with him, effortlessly. It wasn't long before she rode with eyes closed, arms outstretched, trusting, and confident.

She never needed a saddle; he never needed direction; it was as though they were one.

Brooke needed to stand on a bench to brush down her four-footed companion (which she did after every ride), so she was looking down on her father as he ambled toward her and picked up a brush to help. Looking at him from this angle, it struck her; his hair had thinned and grayed, and his shoulders stooped a bit.

Funny, you don't notice how someone ages when you see them every day.

They brushed for a while.

'Doing the work,' is how he'd put it. He was a big believer in making things with his hands; taking the time to figure out how things went together, looking at things from every angle. Doing the work. It was his version of meditation.

"'Seems like you're about ready," he said.

"Two days," she told him. "I'm set. It's getting all those soldiers outfitted and supplied. I guess they have to be ready for anything."

"The less you know, the more you have to prepare," he said.

She looked at his careworn face. "You don't have to worry about me," she reassured him.

"Really?" He shook his head. "You have no idea what you're going up against."

She brushed long strokes down the stallion's back. "Actually, I have a very good idea of what I'm going up against."

He looked at her.

She shook her head, "You don't want to know."

Before he got upset, she reached over the horse's back and grabbed his hand.

"Knowledge is power, right?" she asked him.

He couldn't argue with her. He wanted to.

They went back to brushing.

"I know this sounds like bad fathering, but, I'm not that worried about you," he told her, "doesn't it sound wrong?"

"Oh, my goodness. Yes," she said. "Wait. No. No, it sounds right. Right?"

"Princess, there's no one like you. There never has been," he said. "And that's coming from someone who married your mom. I should know." He stopped brushing. "I want you to remember; you aren't merely a Princess – which is a huge thing."

"Yes," she said, smiling.

"You were conceived with magic inside of you. It's never happened. Someone like you has never happened," he told her. "Whatever conjurers or beasts you come across, they all started off as normal, living beings. You're heading off to find a witch who had to work and train and practice to become one. You are born of magic."

Brooke searched the stables, thinking.

"So don't you let anyone push my little girl around," he told her.

"No, sir," she answered.

"Good," he said and patted her hand. The King turned away suddenly.

He took a few steps and stopped.

"What is it?" Brooke asked, dropping her brush and going to him. "What's the matter?"

He shook his head slightly. "You're going to lift this spell. I know that. It's selfish of me ..." He couldn't quite look her in the face. "Because of it, I've been lucky enough to spend every day of your life with you. Now ..." he took a breath to steel himself and look at his beautiful daughter. "I'm going to miss you, very much."

"Oh, Daddy," Brooke said as she wrapped her arms around his neck. He hugged her.

Neither of them wanted to let go.

❀ ❀ ❀ ❀ ❀ ❀ ❀

"Can I speak to you a minute? Ben?"

He was meditating on his usual perch – the windowsill above the washroom.

"Hello? I would like to talk to you." It was Queen Jessica's voice coming from below.

What was going on?

Benjamin ruffled his feathers, bringing himself around.

"Yoo-hoo," the Queen's voice echoed.

Ben twisted his head to get a proper view of Queen Jessica through the steam.

She motioned with her hand for Ben to come to her. "Come along."

No one had ever disturbed his meditation before, so it was taking the Parakeet Prince a while to get his bearings. And the

Queen was summoning him.

This time, her voice had a tinge of impatience to it. She stressed the word 'can' and annunciated it as though speaking to a child: "You ... *can* ... under ... stand ... me, can't ... you?"

Ben said, "Of course, Your Majesty," and then corrected it to one tweet. He fluttered down through the billowing clouds of steam toward the Queen.

"Ah, good," Queen Jessica said and swept out of the room.

Benjamin caught up with her as she sat on the garden bench.

How majestic she was: every movement, effortless, yet demanding of your attention: poised, not posed.

Queen Jessica patted the stone bench beside her. Ben swooped down and took his place.

"No reason to mince words," the Queen began. "I've established communications with your father. I didn't tell him about you – that would be your prerogative."

Queen Jessica held out her finger, the same way Brooke did. It took Ben by surprise – that the Queen would become so personal. He hopped up and perched on her finger, and she drew him in closer to her face.

"Your father believes you to be dead, Benjamin."

Ben nodded. He figured as much.

"The only person thought to survive the Sorcerer's rage was the Witch, you and Brooke are hoping to find," she explained. "I'm sorry to be the one to tell you, Ben, but two of your brothers set out to find you ... and never returned."

It's difficult to tell in which direction a Parakeet is looking once you understand how much of the world they can see at once (and the Queen did), so she asked him, "Do you understand?"

One quiet tweet.

"As broken-hearted as your father was, he decreed that no one else be allowed to enter the forest – even though it meant he'd never know for sure what became of his youngest and favorite son."

Ben cocked his head this way and that, trying to understand what he was hearing. Favorite son?

"Did you know that's how he felt about you?" she asked him. Two tweets.

"Fathers try never to show favoritism. Being faced with overwhelming grief, it may have been too difficult to hide," she explained.

Ben was grateful he didn't have any tear ducts – it wouldn't be very Princely of him to cry before a Queen.

"With your permission, may I tell your father that you're safe, and all that's happened?" Queen Jessica asked.

Ben tried to tweet. He nodded, instead. The Queen lifted her finger into the air, allowing the Prince to fly away.

Though Brooke didn't mention it, Ben was sure the Queen had told her about his family. Friends know.

He didn't sleep much that night. At one point, he flew over to the skylight and perched on the wooden crossbeam, bathed in moonlight.

He was now invested in this quest as much as his friend was.

❦ ❦ ❦ ❦ ❦ ❦ ❦

On the day of their departure, the giant royal stable doors swung open, and Princess Brooke emerged, caped and hooded, on the back of her high, white charger. As the Parakeet Prince swooped down from the sky, she took her place at the head of a column of two hundred soldiers, led by Lord Hester and his knights-in-training. Every man, woman, and bird committed to challenging a Sorcerer with terrible destructive powers and changing the   destinies (if you believe in that sort of thing) of two kingdoms.

~ *XIV* ~

The Old, Old Man

No one had seen anything like it.

A strange caravan, even in a time of magic: a cloaked Princess riding bareback on a great white stallion, two hundred soldiers, four abreast on horse and foot following, and a snow-white Parakeet with golden feathers on its head, leading them toward the adventure of a lifetime.

The men were ordered not to speak or cause a commotion. Scouts were sent ahead, instructing everyone to remain silent as the procession passed.

That didn't last. If there's one thing people can't do for very long, it is to keep their mouths shut. No matter because the voices and sounds of the world going by folded nicely into Brooke's riding meditation.

They would stop at homes, inns, barns, mills – anywhere the Princess could go inside.

Ben would gingerly slow the horse down to a stop. The steed would bow its head and kneel, allowing Brooke to gently slide to the ground.

As soon as the Princess entered the structure, she would shake off her cloak and get to know the locals.

When she'd introduce Ben, most people thought she was crazy. (Of course, they'd never say so.) Then she'd translate his bird's-eye view of the area, leaving them all dumbfounded.

Who would have thought the real world would be so much more fascinating than a book? She had no idea how much each person would mean to her and how moved she'd be hearing the stories of their lives.

The Princess had dreamt of traveling this road all her life. From the moment she was told of her spell, she began thinking about how she'd track down her jailor and lift it.

When her dreams took flight, so did her imagination.

Brooke was helping a farmer's wife unpack the basket of food and drink she'd brought. "Guests must always bring a gift," the Princess explained when she noticed the woman fretting. "It's the Law. "You wouldn't want me to break the law, would you?"

"Why, no, Your Royal Highness," the woman said.

"You can call me Brooke; that'll be easier," the Princess told her. "Tell me all about your day. I want to hear everything."

The hostess put on some tea. "Why would you want to hear about that?" she asked Brooke. "It's long, hard, and boring. Kind of like that game men play: chess. Tell me, how is that a game?"

"I don't know," the Princess said, smiling. Taking the kettle from her hostess, "I'll do this. I enjoy it. You sit."

The farmer's wife wanted to argue but thought better of it and took a seat at her own table.

"Do you know about me?" Brooke asked her. "What's happened to me?"

"Yes, Your Highness," the wife said, bowing her head.

"Then maybe you can understand," Brooke said, "your boring day is like a dream come true for me."

Brooke was transported, listening to the farmer's wife going on about her day: the stove door she had to kick open sometimes, the little chick who's always late to the feeding, the pleasure her little herb garden gave her.

By the time they had to go, the two were friends.

It was like that at every stop.

❀ ❀ ❀ ❀ ❀ ❀ ❀

Ben was quietly flapping down the road when he sensed something wrong. He spun around to see Lord Hester and the column at a standstill. Brooke and her horse were nowhere to be seen.

The Princess had veered off the road onto a path leading into the woods.

"Any idea where she's headed?" Hester asked Ben as the company armed themselves.

Two tweets.

The Parakeet flew ahead of the Princess to see where she was going. The path continued as far as he could see (and he could see pretty far). He shot higher to get a better look.

Lord Hester ordered foot soldiers into the wood on either side of the path. Hester, his men, and more soldiers followed Brooke.

Ben couldn't see where the path led, from above. In fact, he couldn't see the path at all. Odd. He dove down to the road, and somehow it was as clear as day. He flew ahead, joining Lord Hester, keeping a safe distance from the Princess.

They followed Brooke's horse as it turned off the path into the thick of the forest and found themselves in a clearing with an ancient stone cottage. The house was encircled with strange looking plants, a small pen with animals, and a quiet stream running alongside.

Where did this home come from when a moment ago there were only thick trees? And the clearing – Ben would've certainly seen this from the air.

The men dismounted and searched the edges of the property. Brooke's steed came to a stop. The horse knelt, and the Princess slid to the ground. Ben tapped on the door to the cottage with his beak, and the door swung open. Hester took the lead with a few of his men, clearing the way for Brooke.

The interior of the cottage was three times the size of its outward appearance. There was a blazing fire with a kettle warming and candles of every shape and size burning on the mantle, shelves, and tables.

There were large, pillowy chairs on either side of an overstuffed sofa. A ratty old blanket covered most of the couch, and a black feline propped itself against one arm. Its yellow eyes blinked at the guests.

Another gray cat lazily stretched out on the hearthrug, already bored with the intrusion of armed men – not a care for the fluttering Parakeet.

Brooke removed her hood and looked around. "Mmm, do I smell cocoa?"

"Yes, yes. Welcome, welcome," came the voice of the old, old man from the mouth of the black cat. His head emerged from the sofa where the cat had been, blinking his yellow eyes. Then the rest of him: the cushions of the couch formed his cloak, the fringes of the blanket his hair and beard. By the time he stood (which took a while), his transformation from a couch to old, old man was complete.

"How are you, my dear," he said to Brooke, welcoming her with open arms.

Brooke stepped into his embrace, saying, "If I were any happier, I'd have to be twins."

He chuckled. "You're a delight."

Holding him, Brooke could feel the brittleness of his bones and hear his shallow breath. He could barely stand, so she helped him back down to the sofa – the real one.

"Please, help yourself to some ... Ah ..."

"Cocoa," Brook said, finishing his sentence.

"Yes, do," he said. "None for me."

The room was suddenly filled with the smell of strong chocolate and cinnamon. On the kitchen table, there were mugs for every person in the room. For Ben, a small dish of the sweetest water he'd ever tasted.

"Look at you," the old, old man said, commenting on the light armor, sword, dagger, bow and arrows she was removing. "Aren't you the warrior?"

"Oh, it's all for show," she told him, taking a mug from Hester and making herself at home on the sofa.

"But what a show," the old man said, smiling. "Oh, and you brought the Prince. Your Highness," he said, bowing his head, "How nice to meet you."

Ben landed on the table in front of him, keeping a safe distance and an eye on the hearth cat. "The pleasure is all mine, sir," he said, bowing back.

"I should like a word with you both in private," the old, old man said, barely waving his hand in the direction of Hester and his men.

At once, a thin veil of fog surrounded the three of them. Beyond the fog, the men continued to drink and move about, but very slowly as if treading in thick water.

"Does the pain never let up?" he asked Ben, pointing his old, old finger at the Parakeet's blackened talons.

"It's not so bad," Ben told him.

"It shouldn't be," the man said, shaking his head, eyes closed. The effort or the worry seemed to wear him down – age him, even. "Leave us," he said with another wave of his hand.

Ben, Lord Hester and his men found themselves outside the cottage.

The soldiers' first instinct was to rush back inside, but Ben tweeted loud: two tweets.

"I've been waiting for you," the old, old man said slowly.

"'Sorry if I kept you waiting," she said.

Simply opening his eyes was difficult for the old man now. "I have something for you," he said to Brooke.

She put down her mug, giving him her full attention.

"Not for you, you understand? For you to give ... would you please?" he asked.

The old, old man was slowing down with each word, each movement. Everything was painful for him. It showed in his face and hands: deepening the wrinkles, sagging. He was aging and shrinking right before her eyes.

"Of course," Brooke assured him. She took his feeble hand in both of hers and turned it over. There was a small pouch in it.

"Is there a message to go with it?" she asked.

Slower still. "Inside," he managed to get out, bobbing his old, old finger toward the pouch.

"Oh, no," she said. "Is this another one of those riddles?"

The old, old man wheezed out a laugh, then another.

"I'll find it; don't you worry," she told him. "I love puzzles. You rest now."

The old, old man gently leaned into her arms, growing older, thinner, and smaller with each passing second.

Brooke closed her eyes and repeated the soothing words: "Inside I'm out. Outside I'm in." The old, old man smiled as if the words were a song to him.

Over and over she said them as he slowly faded into dust.

The outline of his body was still there, but now, merely particles of glittery dust, catching the firelight.

Brooke opened her eyes. Taking a deep breath she sucked the shiny particles into her lungs. "Outside I'm in." The particles flowed into her lungs. Repeating, "Inside I'm out." Back out into the room came the sparkling dust. Again. Each time, fewer shiny bits came out. Each time, her skin, eyes, and hair brightened until she became a creature of light.

The cloaked Princess came out of the cottage door holding the round gray cat. She set the animal down on the stoop and closed the door.

Brooke and the soldiers mounted. Riding off without a sound.

Ben lingered behind and watched as the cottage faded, becoming a dull gray dust and floating away in the wind.

The cat shudder-shook the dust off its back and scurried off into the wood.

Ben looked at his newly healed, bright yellow talons, chirped a quick, "Adieu," and flew off.

~ XV ~

The Witch

A storm was moving in. Dark clouds filled the sky.

A crack of thunder split the ears of Brooke's company. The Princess, the Parakeet and the horse vanished.

Hester knew, in keeping with the spell, the Princess would reappear in the last building she'd entered. He led the column back to the inn where they'd stopped for lunch.

Princess Brooke wasn't at the inn. She was in the shack off on a side road they'd put her in, as the company made preparations for the rain. Seated on her horse, she was squished up against the roof. She nearly crushed Prince Ben who had been napping beneath her cloak. After freeing themselves, they made a fire and waited for the soldiers to come.

When the rain stopped, Brooke reckoned Lord Hester must have forgotten about the shack and suggested they go back to the previous stop.

The Parakeet kept fluttering around until Brooke asked him

what was the matter. "We shouldn't be traveling without an escort. It's too dangerous."

"We'll be fine," she said. "We'll meet up with them soon."

"This is my fault. It's all my fault," he tweeted. "I should've never allowed you to make this journey."

"Allowed me?" she said. "That's so adorable."

"Please don't mock me," Ben said. "You have no idea how dangerous the world can be."

"I can handle myself," she told him. "I'm not a child."

"No, you aren't," he said. "You've seen real monsters, but you haven't seen the monstrous cruelty people can inflict on one another. I'm afraid what you think you know keeps you from seeing the truth."

"I know you're concerned about my safety, but–"

"No," he said. He flew closer to her – face to face. "You see more than most, so I'm sure it's obvious to you … I couldn't bear to see you hurt. Without you, 'they' may as well clip my wings and lock me in a cage. You're the reason I soar, Princess."

"Oh, Ben … I guess it's not only your feathers that are soft, huh?"

Ben's little parakeet head moved up, down, and sideways – anywhere to avoid Brooke's smiling eyes. "I've gotten used to you is all. I'd have to train an entirely new enchanted Princess or something."

"Thank you for looking out for me," she told him seriously. "I always feel safe with you."

"'Not sure I'd be much help should danger arise."

"Oh, huh. You're something more powerful than fifty enemies," she told him, "... a true friend." The Parakeet looked at her now. "You're right, of course," she said. "I'll wait here. You can fly up to get a Ben's eye view of the road. When our soldiers show up, we'll go down and meet them. Alright?"

He nodded.

Brooke tossed another piece of wood on the fire.

"The old man," Ben said, "that was Beau's master?"

Brooke nodded.

"How did you know where he lived?"

"I didn't," Brooke told him. "It was all his doing."

"What did he want?" Ben said, "If you don't mind my asking?"

"Not at all," she said. "He wanted to make amends, I think. Healing your feet – which you never told me about, by the way. How can you be suffering and not tell me?"

Ben shrugged his wings.

"Silly bird. That's the last time," she warned him.

"Yes, Your Highness," he said.

She smiled. "He gave me something for Beauregard: a gift with some kind of message. I haven't looked at it yet," she said.

"You ... You haven't looked at it?" Ben got closer to her face. "What have you done with Princess Brooke?"

Brooke laughed.

"Did he give you something as well?" he asked her.

She nodded.

"What was it?"

She looked at her friend. "All he had."

Ben didn't understand. "He would have been a great ally. Can you imagine what we could do if he were with us?"

"He is," Brooke said, more to herself.

The Parakeet ruffled his feathers.

"I know you don't believe in destiny ..." Brooke began.

"Here we go," Ben said.

"Yet, you admit you can't know how a spell works?"

"True," he said.

"So, couldn't magical forces have a sort of fate built into them?" she said. "You and me, maybe everyone touched by Beauregard's sorcery, are tied together somehow? Isn't that possible?"

"Anything's possible," Ben said.

Brooke laughed again. "It would be like we're all part of this odd family. You have to protect your family, right?"

"When presented with a wrong, we're obliged to make it right, if it's within our purview." he said. "Otherwise, we become a party to the offense."

"Exactly," she said, "Only with smaller words. So, I think you just admitted it's our destiny to stop the Sorcerer."

Ben looked at her.

"Right?" she asked. "Destiny? Or is fate a better word?"

"As we've established already, you're the teacher; I'm simply here to learn," he said.

His head cocked to one side, and he took off. Returning a moment later to report seeing the column on the road.

Brooke scratched her great horse's nose and watched the

beast kneel down for her to mount. She grabbed hold of its mane and swung up onto its back.

Ben perched on her shoulder. He spoke quietly in her ear. "If you say our destinies are entwined, that we're fated to be with one another, who am I to argue?"

She glanced at the bird sideways. "If I didn't know better, your fluffy majesty, I'd think you were flirting with me."

"Oh, that's not flirting, Your Highness," he said as he flitted around and around her head. "When I start flirting, you'll know it." Then he took off.

Brooke laughed.

Brooke began her breathing and pulled her hood over her head. "Inside I'm out. Outside I'm in," she repeated. It took awhile for her to withdraw from a world she was so happy to be a part of.

They headed down to the road and fell in line with the company of soldiers, who adjusted quietly, little by little until she and Ben were at the lead.

The following day, as the sun was setting, they came upon the Olde Inn, settled on a wide, rocky ledge jutting out of the base of the mountain.

The clouds were rumbling in the distance, threatening a new storm as our travelers went inside.

❀ ❀ ❀ ❀ ❀ ❀ ❀

Brooke wasn't her normal, chatty self inside the door of the inn. She kept her hood over her head, keeping her face in shadows. Ben perched on her shoulder

She spoke in a hushed tone to Hester, telling him to determine how many men were needed to insure her safety and have the rest make camp away from the inn.

Ben whispered in her ear: "Procure the rooms closest to those occupied by the mysterious tenant."

Brooke nodded. She was about to call the innkeeper over—

"Wait ..." Ben searched the foyer of the inn. "Perhaps you should order something to tweet – I mean, eat. Have the food delivered the same time as the tenant's meal."

"Clever bird," she whispered.

Brooke relayed the instructions to the innkeeper.

Shaking his head, the innkeeper told her, "Miss, I have orders not to disturb the occupant of those rooms."

"Which you will follow," Brooke said, raising her head into the light enough for the man to see her face and crown. "As you will follow mine, with discretion."

"Of course, Your Highness," he said, bowing his head without drawing attention.

He led the Princess, Ben, Lord Hester, and his men down a corridor, lighting lamps as he went. When the innkeeper reached the end of the hall and lit the last lamp, a massive door seemed to jump out of the darkness, surprising the party.

Showing them into the room across from the door, the innkeeper went about lighting lamps and opening windows to let in the night air and the sound of rain. "Not much call to rent these rooms or this side of the inn at all if the truth be told," he said, shaking the dust from the curtains.

Lord Hester examined the room, taking note of the terrain outside the windows.

The Princess and Ben were fixed on the huge door across the hall. Its iron hinges creaked, struggling to hold up under the weight. "Is there a key?" she asked.

"None that I know of, Your Highness," the innkeeper responded. "No keyhole."

Odd.

"If I may, Your Highness …" he said, removing his cap and bowing his head. "There's been them – drunkards without my knowing, or big fellas that drunk their fill of courage – who've done their best to open that door and couldn't budge it an inch."

"We're hoping to be invited in," she told him.

The man looked at her, squinting. "She's locked herself away. Not said a word for years. Could be there's good reason. You may not want to hear what she has to say," he suggested.

"You're probably right," she said, taking his rough hands. "Truthfully, I'm a little frightened of what's behind that door. But my father says you're supposed to listen harder when someone tells you something you don't want to hear."

The man nodded.

"Where is he when you need him, though?" she said, smiling. She patted his hands. "How about that dinner? I'm starving."

"Right away, Your Highness," he said, bowing his way out.

Hester's men had forgotten about the door across the hall when the Princess started speaking. They looked at it again now.

It didn't appear so big anymore.

❀ ❀ ❀ ❀ ❀ ❀ ❀

A crack of thunder made the Princess jump.

The flash of lightning that followed shocked the hallway and door with a blue-white tint, exposing the darkest corners for the blink of an eye, creating an eerie portrait of the scene ...

Ben was on his familiar perch of Brooke's shoulder – she in the doorway of their room, her eyes fixed on the bottom of the forbidden door. Lord Hester and his officers surrounded them at a fair distance. The dinner was sitting in the opening at the base of the door.

Ben shook out a feather from under his wing.

Everyone watched as it casually floated, pendulum-like, to the floorboard.

That's when they saw it ...

A hand. Reaching out to grab a side of the tray. It was ... attractive, Brooke thought – or would be if it had been cared for.

She gasped. The other hand appeared – like that of a corpse, the skin grafted and scarred as though cut and sewn together – what there was of it. Two fingers and the thumb had no covering at all down to the knuckles – skeletal, with tips of long, gray nails.

The hands reacted to the Princess's sudden intake of air with a jolt, and then scrambled to grasp the tray and yank it back into the darkness.

"No, please," Brooke blurted out, rushing to the door. "Forgive me."

She made a fist to bang the door but put her hand on her

forehead, instead, and closed her eyes. "Honestly, I don't deserve it. There's no excuse for my rudeness."

Lord Hester and his men were inching nearer, weapons drawn. One stern look from her sent them back to their positions.

"I ask that you hear me out in any case," she said to the door.

Brooke looked to Ben, still on her shoulder. He encouraged her on with a nod of his head. "My name is Brooke. Princess Brooke. I've come a long way to meet with you. Would you let me in? Please. I need your help and offer my help in return."

A gravelly half-laugh, half-cackle, "Ha," came from inside.

Ben looked at her. Brooke started to say, "I'm not sure what—"

"No," the voice said, cutting her off. "Go away."

Brooke leaned her back against the door, facing Lord Hester.

He motioned to the collection of sledgehammers and iron tools for breaking down the door, displayed in the hallway.

The Princess had told him 'No' when his men brought them in and shook her head 'no' now.

Ben hopped over and perched on the latch of the great door to get his friend's attention. "You know, I can see extraordinarily well in the dark – much better than humans," he told her. "Plus, I can easily fit under this door."

From inside, the crashing of tray and dishes hitting the floor.

"Who's out there with you?" the gravelly voice demanded. "Who is it?"

Confused, Brooke answered as best she could. "It's my parakeet. There are soldiers—"

But the voice cut her off, "Liar."

Catching on, Brooke whispered to Ben, "She can understand you."

"Interesting," Ben whispered.

Brooke chose her words carefully. "My friend is here with me. Is that who you heard?"

This time, the voice had a certain tenderness to it. "What's his name? Tell me," it said.

"His name is Benjamin," Brooke told the door while looking at the Prince, "... but his friends call him Ben."

The massive door came alive: rusted metal grinding, wood creaking, then a blast of stale air rushed into the hallway, sending Ben fluttering toward the ceiling. A crack of blackness appeared.

The heavy door opened.

Before Brooke could step into the darkness, Ben came to roost on her shoulder, and Lord Hester's gentle hand was on the other.

"Even if I allowed you to enter, which I won't," the Princess told Hester, "this is not the time for weapons. In fact ..." Brooke removed her belt, holding her sword and dagger.

"Please, Your Highness," he said. "Reconsider."

"Okay," she said and took the dagger from its sheath, lifted up her skirt, and tucked it into a belt she had strapped to her calf. "Better?"

"No."

"Remember that debt you owe me?" Brooke asked him.

He frowned.

"When we first met?" she said. "You can repay it by staying out." Brooke gave the Lord a peck on the cheek and disappeared into the black hole.

The door creaked shut behind her.

His men watched Lord Hester hit the door with the hilt of his sword, accenting another crack of thunder.

In all their years of training, they'd never seen him upset.

❀ ❀ ❀ ❀ ❀ ❀ ❀

Lightning blasting through the windows of the black room gave the two friends a split-second, brilliant tableau of the room: a wall of heavy curtains and high windows; bookcases with broken shelves and oversized manuscripts; a doorway; the tray with broken dishes strewn across the floor in front of a large table and chairs; behind it, a wash of blacks and shadow forming an arch or a large black hole.

The strike of a match behind them grabbed their attention. They followed the partially covered glow of a candle, moving across the room as a woman, cloaked in black, made her way to the far end of the table against the back wall. Setting the candle down, she leaned back in her chair until she vanished into the shadows.

"Where did she go?" Ben whispered.

"You told me you could see in the dark," Brooke said, through her clenched teeth.

"Did I?" he asked. "Hmm."

The Princess took in a breath and strode across the dark room. Just before reaching the table, she kicked the broken dishes. Recovering, she took a seat at the table.

She readied herself. Determined to remain calm no matter how disfigured the Witch might be. "Are you the one they say? The sole survivor of the Sorcerer's rage?" Brooke asked.

"Obviously not," the Witch said from the darkness.

"Right," Brooke said, glancing at Ben, another survivor. "You lived through it, though?" Brooke added quickly.

"It depends on what you call 'living,'" said the Witch. "Do you know what fire is, Princess?" she asked, as the outlines of her black hood touched the farthest light of the candle. "Do you think it's by chance the Devil paints the walls of hell with flames?"

The Witch's half-corpse of a hand reached out of the black toward Brooke as she rose from her chair. "It grasps the air from your lips, leaving a thick poison in its place."

Brooke clamped her mouth shut as the Witch leaned into the candlelight. Half a head of shocking white hair, laced with streaks of blonde, half a face covered by a clay mask; one wild eye searching. "It seeps into your brain. Like sirens of the sea, it draws you toward a light of pure pain," she told them. "You watch your clothing melt into your skin, breathing flames, setting your lungs on fire from within. You become fire," the Witch yelled across the table.

Suddenly fire erupted behind her, from some deep, unseen cave. Raising her arms, she screamed, "You *are* fire!"

The flames shot forward, surrounding her, outlining her shape but not burning her.

The blast hit Brooke and Ben like a hot tornado, pushing them from the chair.

The clay mask melted from the Witch's face, exposing the bones, tendons, and empty eye socket.

Thunder and lightning electrified the air, shocking Brooke into action. She pressed hard against the wind, yelling back, "You are not! You are not fire!" she told her.

The woman stared at her.

"You aren't destruction," said Brooke. "You've kept it from us."

The Witch looked at the yellow flames around her. "That can be fixed," she said. Reaching back with both arms, she dragged the hotter orange flames from the tunnel.

"No," Brooke screamed.

Ben ducked behind the Princess as the strangling heat filled the room.

The Witch reached back again, pulling red, searing fire in.

"You won't!" Brooke yelled. She grabbed the woman's skeletal hand.

The Witch tried to pull free.

The flames were drawn toward the clasped hands. Heat concentrating – their fingers, hands, wrists glowed red. Burning.

A fireball exploded upward, crashing through the roof, knocking the women back.

The violence of the room slowed. Raindrops sizzled, hitting the table.

"You're not fire," she told the Witch. "You're more ... much more," the Princess said in a calmer, stronger voice, as the wind and fire began to fade. "You have walked through fire. You've mastered it."

The firestorm gone, the Witch collapsed in her chair.

There were banging and loud voices coming from the door.

Brooke yelled over her shoulder that everything was alright.

The candle lit itself, showing the face of the Witch, with the mask restored. "Who are you?" she said. "Why are you here?

"I came because they say you are wise ..." Brooke started.

"Liar," said the Witch. "Never flatter an ugly person. I'm not wise; I'm smart. Smart enough to know you'll never make it to this journey's end."

Seeing the shock on the Princess's face, as though she'd been stabbed in the heart – was too much for Ben. He flew at the Witch's face, set on pecking her other eye out.

"No, Ben," the Princess said.

The Parakeet fluttered in place, considering.

"You tell me why we've come, then," Brooke said.

"You've obviously been cursed," said the Witch. "Both of you." Ben and Brooke looked at each other. "You think I might be able to lift them."

"Really? Is that what you see?" Brooke asked.

The Witch grunted and leaned in to get a closer look. Wait. There was something in the girl's eyes. "No," she said.

"No. Not cursed," the Princess said. "Merely under a spell. We've already found a way around one. What I want ... is for you to join us."

"Join you? What is this, a quest?"

"Yes. To defeat the Sorcerer," Brooke told her.

The Witch laughed. A sort of scratchy, guttural sound – probably better described as a 'cackle'. "You, and what army?"

"The one camped down the hill."

The Witch wasn't laughing anymore. "They won't help much in that forest, sweetie."

"You will, though," Brooke said.

"Oh goodness, dearie," the Witch said, shaking her head. "You're pitiful. Do yourself a favor; go back to your shiny castle where you can sit in front of your dressing table and look at how pretty you are. This isn't a storybook. There's no happily ever after." She banged on the table with her fists. "Do I look like a knight in shining armor? Is this something that should even see the light of day?" Leaning in closer, the rain soaking her half-head of hair. 'You're only here because you need me – you need something from me; ugly, pitiful, disgusting, half-dead, me."

"Yes. We need you," Brooke said. "So do Ben's brothers, swallowed up by the evil forest. His father needs his sons back. All the vanished people need you." Brooke pulled up the sleeve, exposing a patch of burnt skin on her forearm.

Ben's feathers ruffled. Where did that scar come from?

"You aren't the only person who's been through hell," Brooke told her.

"Who are you?"

"You need something from us, too," Brooke told her

"What would that be?" she asked, holding up her corpse-like hand, "A dainty glove?"

"Friends," she told her.

The Witch burst out laughing. "Friends?" She stopped laughing. "Oh, no, you're serious?"

Ben said, "Who else knows you? Understands you? Is connected to you?"

"Do you want to know who I am?" Brooke asked her. "I'm your best hope."

The Witch threw up her hands. "I can't tell which one of you is crazier."

"Hope of a life outside of this room," Brooke continued.

"I guess it's you," the Witch said. "The answer's no. Bye. Get out."

"I've come through fire with you," Brooke added.

"No, your lunacy. No," the Witch told her and sat down, leaning back into the shadows.

"I know you're scared," Brooke said.

"Ha," the Witch croaked from the darkness.

"That shouldn't stop you from doing what you know is right for you and the right thing to do," the Princess said.

Raindrops splashed on the table, forming puddles. Brooke searched the room.

"Well, I should get out of the rain," she said, getting up to go. "Oh, I'm sure you don't care about money or fame, but I should at least mention there's a sizable reward."

"Two Kings' ransoms," Ben added.

"And you'd be hailed a hero, in both lands," she said.

"'Which goes in the history books," Ben said.

"There's a title involved," Brooke said. "Which comes with an estate."

"It does in Athenaeum, as well," Ben said.

"'Just thought you should know," Brooke said. "We have all the details somewhere."

"Not that it matters," Ben said.

"No," Brooke said. "We're staying for a few days. If you have any questions ..."

The Princess and the Parakeet headed to the door. They could barely find it, much less figure out how it opened. Calling back, "How do we ...?"

"Pull. It's unlocked," the Witch's voice yelled back. Then, more to herself: "It's always unlocked."

The Princess opened the door, letting in some much-needed light from the hall. "Have a good evening," she said.

"We'll need the Giant's help," the Witch said.

The Princess and the Parakeet looked at one another. Giants?

"'Sorry?" Brooke said.

When they turned around, the Witch had come out of the shadows. "Giants: two of them. They're the only ones who can bring down the Sorcerer's wall," the Witch said, smiling. (Or as close to a smile as she could get. More like a grimace.) "And you're paying to have my ceiling fixed."

Brooke nodded. "We leave tomorrow then." She smiled and turned to go.

"A countess," the Witch said. "I want to be a countess."

"Very well," Brooke said. With a nod of her head, "See you in the morning, Countess."

Ben bowed his head, "Until the morrow, my lady."

~ *XVI* ~

The Evil Forest

The Princess, the Parakeet, and the Witch didn't make much headway the first day of their journey together. (Let's just say, the Witch had a hard time adjusting.)

Seeing the company of soldiers at the bottom of the mountain, she blurted out, "Wow, you did bring an army."

The Princess was whisked back to the inn.

Later, at a crossroad, she yelled, "Hey! This way's shorter."

Brooke disappeared again.

Over two hundred men looked at the Witch. "Touchy, huh?" she said.

It was suggested the Witch take a position farther back in the column where she'd be free to speak her mind. Brooke insisted they ride side by side.

Ben's solution was to have tents set up every mile or so in advance so Brooke could make short stops – cutting down on the recovery time.

It still took two days to reach the Athenaeum border instead of an afternoon, and another four to arrive at their destination. By the evening of the sixth day they were camped on a hill, overlooking the forbidden forest.

Lord Hester and his men found it hard to look at the burnt, skeletal features of the enchantress. Brooke or Ben kept their eyes fixed on the woman.

They were discussing the best way to breach the wall of bones surrounding the wood when the conversation stopped.

The sounds from the soldiers' campsite below ceased.

There it was. Thunder.

No. Thunder and gnashing? Splintering? Slight tremors.

"What is that?" Squire Moore, one of Hester's students asked.

"That," the Witch said, "is the sound of Giants."

❀ ❀ ❀ ❀ ❀ ❀ ❀

They were sitting around the fire, eating.

Well, not everyone. Brooke was farther away from the fire, under the canopy of her tent. Most of them were watching the Witch eat. Using her skeleton fingers as both knife and fork, alternately: shredding meat from the bone. At one point, she ripped the gray nail off one finger and used the bone tip as a toothpick to extract a stubborn morsel of food.

She looked up to see the disgusted looks on all the faces. "What?" she asked. "It goes back on." She reattached the ugly nail. "See." She took a drink. "You know, you can't take all those soldiers into the woods," the Witch said.

"Why not?" Lord Hester asked.

"Because they'll be eaten."

"Good point," the Princess and the Parakeet said together. Brooke smiled at him. No one could say if he smiled back or not.

"I may be able to protect you and the bird, here," the Witch explained, "... but not two hundred soldiers."

"These men can take care of themselves," Lord Hester told the woman.

The Witch cackled. "Who are you again?" she asked. "And why are you so stupid?"

"Please," Brooke said to the Witch.

"Oh, right. Manners," the Witch said. "Pardon me."

"The Princess goes nowhere without a guard," Lord Hester said.

"Right. Well, you shouldn't go either, missy," the Witch said to Brooke. "You can't do anything, anyway. Stuck indoors. You tricked me. I wouldn't've come if I knew you were so useless."

All the men stood and faced the hag. Ben fluttered in her face.

"Ooo, scary men," she said, sticking a piece of meat with her finger bone. "And a little Princely appetizer." She chomped at Ben like she was going to bite him.

Ben darted backward.

"Sit down, boys," she said, "or I'll have one of you for dessert."

"I'm going in," Brooke told her. "You can't do it alone. If you could, you would've done it already."

The Witch shook her head, saying, "I've never met anyone so stupid, so cursed, and so full of hope."

Brooke smiled, and then began laughing to herself. Then she burst out laughing.

"What? What is it?" the Witch demanded.

The Princess tried to speak, but she was laughing so hard that she bent over from the ache in her stomach.

Ben chirped in, "She named her horse, 'Hope', so 'Hope' is always with her," he explained.

"And it's not ..." Brooke started but burst out laughing again. Then she turned to Ben, "Why is this so funny?" Back to the Witch, wagging her finger at her, playfully reprimanding her, "It's not a curse ..." Waving to Ben to join her, together they said, "... It's a Spell."

With that, Princess Brooke fell on the ground, laughing, as Ben flittered above her, tweeting (or laughing – it's hard to say which).

❀ ❀ ❀ ❀ ❀ ❀ ❀

The next morning, the mood was decidedly different.

Soldiers were at work by dawn, clearing the mountain of bizarre bones from the road. Fear crept deeper into the men's hearts with each new monstrosity. They were more than happy to allow Lord Hester and his men to lead.

"Make way for the Princess," a voice called from the back of the company. Soldiers opened a path.

"This I gotta' see," the Witch said.

"Make way for the Princess," the Squire Moore yelled out. He was holding the reins of a team of horses, pulling a large supply wagon. The carriage had been refashioned as a kind of fortress, a heavy, wooden, rectangular box. Doors were opened wide on every side by knights-in-training. In the center, Princess Brooke stood, dressed for battle, her bow in hand.

The soldiers cheered.

"She knows how to make an entrance; I'll give her that," the Witch said.

"I would not ask a single man to put his life at risk, if I was not willing to do the same," Princess Brooke told the crowd. "Today, let us burn a path through the evil that has grown unabated for far too long and build a road, free of corruption."

The soldiers cheered.

Brooke dipped the tip of her arrow into a cauldron, lighting it on fire. The squires did the same. They all let loose the arrows, straight ahead, into the thick of the evil forest.

Overhead, a hundred more flaming arrows sailed toward the wood.

Screams and cries pierced the company's ears as the wood lit up.

Brooke and the toxophilites shot off round after round of burning projectiles.

"Bring your fire," the Princess yelled to the Witch.

Hester and his men gave the Witch plenty of room as she summoned her power.

"Like sirens of the sea, it draws you toward a light of pure pain," she said, eyes closed in a low, guttural growl. "Your skin melts, breathing flames, your lungs on fire. You become fire."

Flames caught hold of her cloak.

Soldiers ran toward her, to save her, but Hester's men held them back.

"You *are* fire!" Raising her arms, the Witch screamed, "I am fire." She pulled the flames over her head, sending them into the trees.

The world around them erupted into a nightmare inferno. Tortured cries of beasts filled the air – stampeding toward the army, still aflame. Dropping at the forest's edge. Freakish plants gushing black ooze, shriveling in the heat.

Horses reared up. Soldiers stood their ground.

As the fire raged, every man, woman, and bird averted their eyes. No living thing deserved an end like that.

The jungle was far too dense and humid to burn very long. When the smoke cleared, a wide tract of black earth, smoldering skeletons, and debris extended a hundred feet into the wood.

The Witch had fallen to her knees and remained there, unable to witness the destruction she'd unleashed.

Brooke had her brought to her wagon, where she gently washed the soot from the woman's face and arms. "I didn't know it would be like this," Brooke admitted. "I'm sorry."

"Shut up," the Witch said without looking. Mocking her, "Oh, I didn't know fighting devils would be so dirty." She looked at her now, with her wild eye, and spoke with her darkest voice, "Well, my perky Princess, we're just getting started."

"I guess," she said, nodding. Brooke searched the blackened road into the forest. "It's the beginning ... of the end."

Ben insisted he be the first to scout the burnt forest, being the quickest and most aware of its dangers.

"It appears the fire has terminated the growth of the forest," he reported to Brooke on his return. "As is true with the perimeter of the wood, no plant or creature venturing beyond the jungle's confines can survive."

"How come it doesn't grow anymore?" Brooke asked him.

"Because it's dead," the Witch said, with her back to the group.

"Yes," Ben said, "I happen to agree with our resident ... er ... fire countess ... What is your name, by the way?" he asked the Witch.

"Oh, didn't I tell you?"

"No, actually," Ben said.

"It's Shut-up-and-mind-your-own-business," she told him.

"Ah." Ben went back to Brooke. "The forest is self-contained. It feeds off itself – an endless cycle of mutations. By scorching the earth, we're eliminating the fertilizer it needs to repopulate."

"What did he say?" Lord Hester asked the Princess.

"Uh ... Fire kills it," she said.

"Let's get to it, then," he said and headed out with the men.

Brooke turned to Ben, "Did I get that right?"

He shook his head.

"It didn't quite have the scientific flair you bring to it," she said, "But I think I–"

"You're incorrigible," Ben said as he flew off.

Another assault took them deeper into the wood.

Brooke could see that summoning that amount of firepower was taking its toll on the Witch. She looked into the creeping jungle all around her. So many strange cries. Voices … telling her …

Brooke ordered Lord Hester to call an end to the day.

"One more," the Witch said and went off on her own.

"You've done enough," Brooke yelled after her. "More than enough."

The Witch spun around, pointing her skeleton finger, "You don't rule over me, perky," she yelled back. "I'll blister this whole kingdom if I choose."

Brooke held her stare. Then nodded. "Very well, Countess," she said. "We'll muster the troops and follow your lead."

Brooke turned to Hester and Ben. "How can we best protect her and ourselves if things don't go as planned?"

Ben advised bringing the archers to the front after their volleys.

"My men and I will be at her side and yours, Princess," Hester added.

"Okay," she said.

"If I may, Your Highness?" Lord Hester asked.

Brooke nodded.

"If we feel it's a mistake to go forward, why are we?" he asked.

"She's our friend," Brooke explained. "We support her, no matter what."

Lord Hester bowed and went to work.

Everyone went to work: soldiers arming themselves, horses cleared, carts loaded and unloaded with supplies; swords, spears, and daggers being sharpened; shields tested.

Brooke and Ben were in the wagon. She searched the forest for answers. "You know, this is the first day in years I haven't meditated."

"Me, too," Ben said.

They looked at each other.

"I'm afraid, Ben," she whispered.

"Me, too."

"What do you say we shut these doors and take a little time to breathe?" she asked him. "Whatever happens next, I'd like to live it with clarity ... and with you."

"Me, too."

When Princess Brooke reopened the doors of her wagon some twenty minutes later, she and the Parakeet Prince were as ready as they would ever be to battle the forces of evil.

Which, as it turns out, wasn't nearly enough.

~ *XVII* ~

The Fires Of Promena

J t began the same as the other assaults: Brooke and the knights in training sending flaming arrows deeper into the wood, the archers filling the sky with more. Volley after volley.

"Bring your fire," the Princess yelled to the Witch.

The Witch went through her preparations.

A hundred archers moved to the front, bows ready. They surrounded the Witch, the wagon, the soldiers, and squires.

Flames caught hold of the Witch's cloak. Raising her arms, she screamed, "I am fire." As she was pulling the flames over her head, there was a crack of a tree falling just beyond the tree line – a massive one.

It must've caught fire during one of the earlier assaults and had been burning for hours. When it gave way, it took all of the trees in its path along with it. There were so many, and the large tree was so thick, they didn't disintegrate in the clearing. They landed only a few feet from the Fire Witch, shaking the ground.

The impact unleashed a flurry of long-needled hornets, stinging the Witch all over, before burning up in her flames.

"No, no," Brooke said.

"Oh, no," Ben said from the air above.

With a huge effort and a gut-wrenching scream, the Witch tried to drag the fire over her head. But it was too much for her crippled body, and she fell backward, waving her arms as she did.

"Everyone, down," Hester yelled. Most of them were already seeking cover.

As her arms flailed, the fire-stream whipped through the forest like a hot knife: slicing trees in all directions.

A corner of Brooke's roof caught fire.

Hester's men were the closest to the Witch and first to react. With no thought for their own safety, they managed to smother her flaming hands and kill off the remaining hornets.

Red and purple welts were bubbling up on her skin where she'd been stung.

For a few moments, there was quiet. Everyone kept their movements small, stepping back, little by little. Maybe the damage wasn't so bad.

Then another enormous crack. Another. Another. Wood splintering.

"Archers close in. Form a perimeter," Lord Hester ordered. "Squires. The Princess and the Witch."

Another tree fell. "Bring her to me," Brooke ordered the squires who were caring for the Witch.

The ground shook as a tree hit – knocking people off their feet. Another – crushing soldiers. Another. The trunks laid a new foundation of fertilizer over the scorched earth.

The evil forest of Promena was fighting back.

Squire Moore jumped from the wagon and grabbed the horses' reins to turn them around. His job was to collect the Witch and get her and the Princess to safety.

They came – from every direction: throngs of deformed animals, reptiles, birds, and insects.

"Fire at will," Lord Hester yelled.

Brooke, the squires, and archers unleashed masses of flaming arrows, filling the air with streaming fire, taking down the first line of advancing monsters.

"Pull back," Hester yelled out. The front line retreated and reformed. "Spears cover the ground. Swords protect the body. Squires roam for stragglers. Arrows to the sky."

Archers tilted up to find flocks of grotesque, winged monsters attacking. Some dissolved over scorched earth, but the smell of blood was driving the jungle demons into a frenzy, and they kept coming.

Brooke let go arrow after arrow as the wagon turned.

Ben was swooping and picking off flying insects from above. Spotting a new danger, he tweeted a piercing cry.

Translating, Brooke yelled out, "Keep your feet moving. Watch the vines."

Charging from every branch and twig, like a nest of vipers,

hundreds of coiling vines advanced on the company. Screams of soldiers dragged into the wet darkness of the forest, strangled and struck by venomous thorns.

Grasping a creeping menace in one hand, splitting it down the middle with his dagger, Lord Hester shouted, "Get the Princess to safety."

"Hold," Brooke told her squire, releasing a flaming arrow into the breast of a wolf-faced eagle diving straight at her. "Hurry, please," she yelled to squires lifting the unconscious Witch into the back of the wagon.

One squire screamed and was dragged out of sight. Brooke unleashed an arrow, pinning the serpentine crawler before it could pull him into the jungle.

A flurry of twisting tentacles invaded the wagon from the other side. The squires sliced off vine after vine, only to have another growth take its place.

A howl brought Brooke's attention back to the wolf-faced eagle, its body blazing, renewing its attack. Arrows shot into it from every side, but didn't slow it down.

Brooke pushed the two squires in the wagon into the corner, out of harm's way and braced for impact.

Ben's hard beak hit the wolf-eagle's eye dead center. It filled the air with a howl-screech and crashed into the wagon's wheel, setting it ablaze.

From the rear, the water brigade went to work.

From the front, hordes of grotesque insects scrambled over the carcasses and corpses, killing one another to be first in line to feast on human flesh.

"Front line," Hester yelled out. "Retreat and reform."

The line of soldiers moved back ten yards, and then formed another line, yelling out, "Huh!"

"Make way," Hester ordered.

Across the front line, soldiers stepped aside, and large wooden barrels were rolled toward the teeming mass of bug monsters.

"Again," Hester yelled out. "Retreat and reform." The soldiers obeyed. "Nets, at the ready," Hester yelled. "Archers light."

Thousands of giant centipede-spiders, spitting wolf-roaches, and swarms of three-horned wasps were bearing down.

"Hold." Buzzing and clamping pincers grew closer. "Hold." The insect army blanketed the barrels.

"Nets," Hester commanded.

Tight woven fishing nets flew over the front line, taking down the flying killers and trapping the crawling ones.

"Archers fire."

Blazing arrows riddled the wooden barrels.

"Quick retreat," Lord Hester ordered.

The front line backed up quickly, without breaking.

The first barrel of oil exploded.

"Cover," he yelled.

Everyone hit the ground.

Barrel after barrel went up in flames.

Sizzling, crackling, screeching cries of pain filled the air.

A splash of water brought the Princess back. She could hardly breathe. The smoke?

The wagon was burning all around her. There were inches of water on the floor.

She was choking.

She tried to look around but couldn't move her head. Brooke was lifted into the air by her neck. She grasped the vine coiled around her throat. Tightening.

Her dagger cut into it. For a second, she could breathe, but then another vine took its place. One more bound her wrist before her dagger could strike. She reached for her sword, but the vines were quicker. Whipping around and around her body, pinning her arms.

Her vision became blurry. Through the front of the wagon, she could make out horses running away and a crowd of soldiers tossing buckets at the wagon until a wall of fire obscured the action.

She was losing consciousness. She closed her eyes – not to welcome death – but to center herself. Her thoughts settled: "Inside I'm out. Outside I'm in."

Brooke dropped her head backward, and her airway cleared for a moment. Even the smoky air was better than none. She exhaled toward the front door. The breath was thick with glittering particles. Widening as it dispersed, it created a hole in the flames.

She watched a hooded figure running toward the wagon. Jumping through the opening.

Pulling the soaked blanket from his head, squire Moore drew

his sword and dagger and carved the writhing plant to pieces.

The Princess ripped away the still wriggling remnants and tossed them into the fire.

"Get them out," she told the squire, nodding to the still-breathing squires in the corner. She went to the unconscious form of the Witch huddled near the back of the wagon.

Moore handed the squire's bodies through the opening in the flames.

The Witch was alive, but not responding.

"You're next, Your Highness," Moore said. "I'll take her."

She smiled at him, shaking her head. "I can't go outside," she told him.

A roar echoed through the forest.

Squire Moore kicked open the fragments of the back wall of the wagon, and they could see the army reforming a front line, the blazing oil fires beyond.

The thunder of massive hooves approaching. Another roar.

Something was charging. Something large.

"More oil," Lord Hester ordered. "Spears to the front. Archers ready."

New barrels of oil were rolled into the flames. Archers lit their arrows and aimed toward the unknown.

Pounding. Closer. Tremors. Ground shaking.

A hundred foot demon stepped out of the murky jungle, hungry for flesh.

A deafening roar as the spittle from its whale-sized, drooling jaw, soaked Brooke's army with burning ooze.

Popping out of the monster's blotchy, alligator hide, were disfigured animal heads, hungry jaws, claws, stingers, and talons, barking, screaming, clutching, and flailing.

The evil forest had thrown all of its gruesome mutations together to create an atrocity hell-bent on defeating the human invaders.

"Wake up, wake up," Brooke demanded of the Witch, as she yanked the exposed stingers from her skin. Puss spitting out of the wounds.

The Princess slapped her, jarring her to attention.

Shaking her head to see more clearly, "What happened? Where are we?"

"We need your help," she told her.

"What else is new," the Witch said.

"We have to get her out," Brooke told the squire.

The squire opened his mouth to speak. A green tongue unraveled.

"No!" Brooke yelled, grabbing her sword.

The vicious vine lashed around Moore and yanked his body back, smashing his limp body up against the wall, breaking through and vanishing into the trees.

"Fire at will," Hester yelled.

Archers filled the air with flaming projectiles: setting fire to the beast, but not slowing him down.

The behemoth stretched its massive jowl, aiming for the

front line of soldiers. The men held their ground. Archers and spearmen sending projectiles into its mouth.

A barrel exploded, knocking it back. Another exploded.

It clawed at its scaly, burning face.

"I need your fire," Brooke said, grabbing the Witch and pulling her up to see the monster.

"I can't," the weak woman said. "I can't."

"You have to. I'll help you," Brooke said, clasping the Witch's boney hand in her own. "You are fire. We are fire."

The beast ripped and clawed the burning skin from its face, unleashing a downpour of black-red blood on the men below. It roared to open sky, and once more at his enemies, then dove at them: claws out, open mouthed.

A huge fireball shot out from Brooke's burning wagon, hitting the monster full in the face.

Another fireball hit it square, knocking it backward.

One more, and the demon exploded in flames. Again, and it fell back into the forest.

The soldiers cheered.

Brooke held the Witch in her arms, lying back in the puddle of water on the floor of the wagon where they could still breathe.

Water came in from the roof and what was left of the walls.

Brooke covered the Witch with her body as water rained down.

"Now they're trying to drown us?" the Witch said, groggily.

The wagon was yanked hard in one direction, then the other. The whole wagon dropped fast, slamming down.

"Ow," the Witch said. "Hey."

"Princess?" Lord Hester's voice cried out.

The two women sat up and looked around.

They were on the ground.

The walls were charred and barely standing. The ceiling was dripping wet. She saw the wagon wheels being dragged away by grappling hooks. Lord Hester, his men and soldiers surrounded them: their skin and clothing were bloodied, burnt, and blackened from fire.

Helping the Witch up, "Get her to a doctor, please. Right away," she said.

"I'm fine," the Witch said.

"I've got her," a squire said, lifting her into his arms. The same squire who'd stopped the flames from consuming the Witch and brought her to her wagon – the same one who was almost dragged off by the vine.

"What are you doing?" the Witch said, wriggling. "Put me down."

"I gotcha'," he said.

"You drop me and I'll turn you into a warthog," she said before passing out.

Many hands reached in to help Brooke to her feet. She refused.

The Princess picked up her sword and dagger, sheathing them both. "Lord Hester," she said grabbing the rest of her equipment. "I'll need my cloak and my horse." Her bow secure across her body, she slung a quiver of arrows over one shoulder.

"At once, Your Highness," he said and dispatched men to do it.

Feeling dressed again, she took a big breath and said, "Now ... Where's Ben?"

When no one answered, she looked around at all the faces.

None would return her gaze.

~ *XVIII* ~

The Giants

Once inside the tent, Brooke removed her cloak. The field hospital they'd set up only had room for the fatally wounded. There were many – all under her command.

She felt Lord Hester's gentle hand on her shoulder, "He's in the back," he told her.

Brooke nodded. She blinked away her tears and started walking. It was torture. She was so anxious to see Ben and so scared of what she'd find. Rows of soldiers: every step, another at death's door because of her.

"We don't have a bird doctor, Your Highness," the nurse explained. "We did the best we could."

Using a bedpan and soft towel, they'd made a little bed for Ben. The nurse pulled back the cloth.

Brooke covered her mouth with her hand, stifling a cry but not the tears that went with it.

His little body ... The only white remaining was the bandages wrapped around his injuries – even they had blood seeping through. Both wings blackened, broken – most of the feathers burnt. His eyes were open, but still, like tiny marbles. He went into convulsions, and Brooke cried out.

Lord Hester returned with some food and drink at dinnertime. He came again as the camp was going to sleep to find she hadn't touched either. He told her that the witch was doing fine. She would fully recover. "She's a hard one to kill," he said.

Brooke smiled and nodded.

When Hester came back a few hours later, he found the Princess asleep on a cot, with her best friend cupped between her hands, inches from her face.

He put a blanket on his Princess and kissed her forehead.

❀ ❀ ❀ ❀ ❀ ❀ ❀

It was nothing like any dream she'd had before. She was herself, doing the same horrible walk through the medical tent ... only worse, because the bloody and burnt soldiers spoke to her as she passed.

A soldier with half his face wrapped in bandages, told her, "I'm not gonna make it." He started coughing and stopped moving. He died with his eyes open, staring at her.

Another soldier told her, "Something bit me in the leg. It really hurts." He pulled back the blanket, and both of his legs were gone.

Squire Moore was sitting at the edge of his cot. When he saw Brooke, he said, "Your Highness. For a while, I didn't think we were going to make it out of there." He grabbed his throat.

"Could you ask the nurse to go get me something? It feels like my throat is—" His chest started heaving. He made sounds like he might throw up.

He coughed up a huge vine. It split into dozens of tentacles and spread throughout the tent: diving down some patients' throats, picking up other men and slamming them to the floor.

A vine came right at her. Brooke reached for a weapon, but she was in her nightgown.

The tip of the vine became a large sunflower. Its center grew teeth, opened its mouth, roared in her face, and dove at her. She screamed, closing her eyes.

When the Princess opened her eyes, everything was peaceful and quiet. Again, she found herself walking through the tent. The soldiers were sleeping now.

She walked down to the last cot, where she'd been resting, and there was a man, sleeping on his side, facing her. She couldn't tell who he was.

Drawing closer, she saw the man had no nose, mouth or ears – only two dead marble eyes.

There was something moving under the covers behind him. The blanket fell away, and he had two blackened, bloody wings.

"Oh, Ben," she said. Brooke was about to run away crying but stopped herself. She turned back to the broken, faceless Ben.

Brooke went back to the cot and gently folded the injured wings back, pulled up the blanket and tucked him in.

She sat on the floor so she'd be eye-level with her faceless friend. She ran her fingers through his hair and hummed a little song.

Brooke leaned her head back, opening her throat wide, pulling in all the air from the room. When she blew out the air, it was filled with golden particles. She aimed them where Ben's mouth should be.

The particles went to work, creating a mouth and nose for him.

Ben breathed the particles into his lungs and began to move. They kept trading breaths and golden flakes.

His eyes came alive. He stretched his shoulders, and two beautiful, golden-white wings spread out. The new Ben recognized his best friend's face in front of him and smiled.

Brooke smiled back and stood up to face the hospital patients. She took in deep breath after deep breath, expelling the golden particles throughout the room. The flakes healed, repaired, and patched up all the soldiers.

Brooke felt a tug on her hand. Ben pulled her down onto the cot.

She lay there, facing him, and cupped his handsome face in her two hands.

They fell asleep looking into each other's eyes.

🏵 🏵 🏵 🏵 🏵 🏵 🏵

The Princess woke with a start. Her hands were empty: no human Ben, no Parakeet Ben. She spun around, searching the room. What happened? Where could he be?

Oh. Was she dreaming again?

The room was so different. Lighter. Brighter. Soldiers were

sitting up, talking to one another. Some were walking around. There was a group of soldiers gathered near the entrance. Lord Hester was with them, smiling, happy.

Ben, in all his snow-white glory was perched on Hester's shoulder.

"Ben," she whispered.

As if he heard her, Ben turned in Brooke's direction.

She stood up.

At the same time, everyone else in the tent turned toward her.

The soldiers, nurses, and doctors knelt and bowed their heads. Lord Hester knelt, smiled and bowed his head.

Then Ben bowed his.

❀ ❀ ❀ ❀ ❀ ❀ ❀

"This is the sword of a hero," Princess Brooke told the crowd, holding up the blade. She stood beneath a canopy at the mouth of her tent, overlooking the entire company. The Witch was on one side, Lord Hester on the other, the squires all around, Ben on her shoulder. "It belonged to my friend: a squire who gave his life to save mine ... as many of our brothers have. They will not be forgotten – not a single man ..." Brooke looked down, taking the moment she needed.

"Though not soon enough to show my gratitude, I have bestowed a knighthood on the former squire, as I will to every squire who stands with me here."

Cheers erupted.

She raised the sword above her head. "Every fallen soldier's name will be etched in the steel of this blade ..."

More cheers.

"And from this day forward, I will carry the sword of Sir Moore with me into battle."

Cheers and applause.

Lord Hester nodded to Brooke in thanks.

The Witch shook her head. "Yeah, give everybody a title."

Ben whispered in Brooke's ear, "Have them bring your carriage around now."

Brooke spoke quietly to Lord Hester. He nodded and collected his men. All except one: the same (now) knight who looked after the Witch during the battle.

"Your little friends are leaving," the Witch pointed out to him. "Should you be running along?"

"I'm to remain by your side," he told her.

"Are you kidding?" The Witch followed Brooke into her tent. The Princess was suiting up.

"I don't need Sir Nursemaid here, looking out for me," she told Brooke.

"Wasn't my idea," the Princess told her. "He volunteered."

"Why?"

Brooke shrugged

"Perhaps, he wished to remain on your good side," Ben suggested. "The side that doesn't shoot out fireballs, that is."

Brooke swung her bow over her head.

"Is everything alright, Perky?" the Witch asked the Princess.

"Truly," said Brooke, with the smallest hint of tears swimming in her green eyes, "Who could expect 'everything' to be alright?"

"Listen," Ben said.

Everyone stood still.

It was far off at first. Distant thunder.

"They're coming," Benjamin said.

More thunder. Growing closer. Voices outside. Everyone heard it that time.

A new wagon pulled up in front of the tent as Princess Brooke emerged.

The thunder was getting closer.

The ground shook as the caravan headed down the scorched, cleared road deeper into the forest. The Knight and the Witch drove while Brooke remained in the wagon with the doors open on all sides. Lord Hester and his band of knights surrounded the carriage on horseback.

More thunder. Wood splintered. Horses grew skittish.

Then they saw the scraped and bloody legs and feet of two approaching Giants. It wasn't until the trees were pulled apart by two sets of thick, gnarled hands that they looked up and saw that the Giants were women – over forty feet tall.

Their bodies were covered in animal skins patched together, creating makeshift smocks; their skin was hard, blistered, caked with mud and blood; their hair, nothing more than birds' nests, and something was wrong with the features of their faces: as though looking at one's reflection in a broken mirror.

The air was thick with silence as they stood. You could hear their wheezing breath.

Brooke swallowed and opened her mouth to speak.

The taller Giant beat her to it. Slurring her words as if her tongue didn't quite fit her toothy mouth, she said, "Why don't you all come into the foresst a bit?"

"The forest isn't exactly our friend," Brooke said to them. "You're welcome to join us."

"Oh, very clever," the smaller one said. "You think we're gonna burn up like all them monsters, don't you? You watch yourself, little Princess."

"I thought no such thing," Brooke said. "I mean you no–"

"Why iss it they got you in a cage?" the taller Giant said, interrupting.

"It's not a cage," Brooke explained.

"Alright a boxx that lookss like a cage," the taller one said. "You have ssmart mouth ass well, don't you? Iss that why they've locked you up, Princcesss?"

"Yeah, that's why exactly," the Witch told them. "It doesn't seem to help, though – she just keeps talking. You should get along great since no one seems to be able shut up around here."

The Giants stepped closer. "What did you ssay?" the taller one bellowed.

"Are you going to eat us, or what?" the Witch said, "I'm getting bored."

"Enough!" the smaller Giant yelled, reaching toward her.

"No," the taller Giant yelled, pulling the other back.

The group backed up as the Giant's hand shot forward.

"Ow, ow, ow!" she yelled, grabbing her hand back as it cleared the tree line. Her scream echoed through the forest. The taller Giant brought her to the ground, breaking trees, shaking the earth as they landed, sending creatures scattering and screeching.

The smaller Giant cried.

The taller one yelled at the group, "Ssee what you've done?"

"I'm sorry," the Princess said, "we meant no harm."

"Iss that ssuppossed to make it better?" the Giant shot back at her. She roared at the group, reached her hand out, right past the trees and scooped the Witch up.

The Knight jumped from the wagon and caught hold of the Giant's finger. Hanging on with one hand, he pulled his dagger and began stabbing her hand as he swung through the air.

"What'ss thiss then?" the Giant said, watching him. "You're gonna hurt yoursself, sson." And she flicked him off.

"Please ladies, don't eat her," Brooke begged them.

"What do you keep going on about eating people?" the shorter Giant asked.

"We're not cannibalss," the other said.

"That's not entirely true, dear," the shorter Giant corrected. "Remember ...? Gertrude?"

"Oh, yess, that'ss right," said the taller one. "I didn't really count her. She was so mean."

"She was," the short Giant shared with everyone. "Mean as spit, that one."

"I thought sshe'd be tougher," the taller said.

"Tougher to chew, you mean?"

The taller Giant nodded, trying keep from laughing.

"Oh, you're terrible," her shorter friend said. Then they both burst out laughing.

"Ladies," the Witch yelled at them.

"Yes, sorry," the shorter Giant said, calming down.

"So you don't eat people ... much ..." the Witch said.

"Let'ss jusst ssay, not too often," the tall Giant said.

"Some people are just askin' to be chewed up and spit out. Know what I mean?" the short Giant asked the group.

"Great. And one of you can leave the forest but the other can't?" the Witch asked.

"Well, the thing iss, we can both leave, actually," the taller Giant explained. "We finisshed growing, ssee? Don't need the foresst."

"Just didn't have anywhere to go," the other said. "Not like we can go have a cup of tea at the inn."

"But your hand," Brooke said to the smaller Giant.

"Oh, right. I didn't really hurt myself," the Giant confessed. "I was playacting."

"Sso, no harm done," the taller one told them.

"Not hurt," the smaller one added.

"Yesss, I ssaid that already," the taller one said.

"I know, I was just reassuring them," the other said.

"But you don't have to, becausse I did that."

"Well, I wasn't just trying to help."

"Repeating what I ssaid iss confussing, though," the tall Giant told her.

"Hey," the Witch yelled at them. "Cut it out."

"Sorry," the smaller Giant said.

The tallest Giant addressed the Witch, saying, "You ssurvived the ssorcerer'ss flamess."

"Barely," the Witch replied.

The shorter Giant motioned to Princess Brooke. Showing her buckteeth, she said, "You didn't seem to suffer much."

Brooke started to say. "Oh, I wasn't–"

"Not you, you idiot," the shorter Giant yelled, interrupting. "The bird."

"Don't call her an idiot," the taller one said. "You don't know if sshe'ss ass sstupid as sshe looks."

"She's here, isn't she?" the short one fired back. "Coming up against giants with nothing but a pretty face. Not the sharpest weapon in the armory, certainly."

"Um ... I–" Benjamin yelled out to get their attention. "I was very lucky, I suppose," he told them.

"Except that you're a bird," the shorter one said.

"Good point," the Witch said.

Hester leaned closer to Brooke, "They can understand the Prince as well?"

"We're all connected," Brooke told him. "Magic."

"Why would you come back?" the taller Giant Woman said to the group, shaking her huge head.

"What would make you to return?" the shorter one echoed.

"I already ssaid that," the taller Giant told the other. "Why musst you alwayss repeat what I ssay."

"I don't always repeat what you say."

"You jusst did it again," she said.

"When?"

"Ladies," Brooke called out to them.

"What!" they both said, turning back to her.

"We've come back to find the Sorcerer," the Princess explained. "And stop him."

The two Giants looked at each other.

"You're going to kill him?" the taller Giant asked.

"No," said Brooke.

"Yes," said the Witch.

"Can we eat him?" the smaller Giant asked.

"What? No," Ben said.

"Only the weak seek revenge," the Princess told them. "The strong forgive."

The Giants looked at each other ... then burst out laughing.

"No wonder they keep you in a cage," the smaller one said. "You're a crazy one."

"We're going to burn a road, to the Sorcerer's tower," Brooke said. "You can join us or be left behind."

"You want uss to join you?" they said together.

"Yes, very much," Benjamin piped in. "We need your help to detweet the Sorcerer. I mean, defeat him."

"Just agree," the Witch confided in them. "Trust me; you're going to, one way or the other."

The two Giant women looked at each other, then at the group.

"We'll help you," they said together.

The smaller Giant leaned in a bit and whispered in a Giant sort of way, "We still get to eat him, though, right?"

~ *XIX* ~
Sisters

urning a road through the Promena Wood took its toll. Destroying life, no matter how evil, is hard on the soul. These beasts were innocent animals and birds at one time – plants and insects simply carrying out their part in the circle of life.

With the Giants' help, the work was easier, but still a daily grind. The ladies would knock down and rip up trees, clearing as much of the forest as they could. Brooke and the Witch would combine forces to send fireballs down the path.

The nights, as nights have always been, were filled with stories.

There were matching campfires on either side of the tree line. Brooke and her army in the clearing, roasting meats and pouring ale. The Giants on the edge of the jungle with skewers of misshapen monsters (often in the tortured throes of death) cooking over an open flame.

Brooke from the mouth of her tent told her story about how the Sorcerer put a spell on her, much the same way as her mother told it to her. She went on to tell them the events that brought her here (leaving out the details of the old, old man's final moments).

When Brooke spoke about her dreams in the forest, the Giants chimed in. "That's how we knew you was royal, you was in our heads," the smaller Giant said.

"Ssnoopin' around in our brainss, keeping uss up at night," the taller one said.

"Snoopin' and sneakin'," the smaller one added.

"Didn't I jusst ssay that?" the tall Giant asked the small one. "Why are you alwayss repeating everything?"

"I'm not," the shorter one argued. "You said snoopin' but you didn't say sneakin'. I added the sneakin'."

"It'ss the ssame thing," the taller Giant told her. "Sso you repeated it twicce."

"More like one and a half, I'd say," the small one said. "One was an exact copy, but the other–"

"Ladies," the Witch yelled out.

"What?" they said together.

Seeing all the scowling faces, the taller Giant said, "Oh. Right. Ssorry."

"You've been poking around in my head, too, eh Princess?" the Witch accused Brooke.

"Not on purpose," Brooke explained. "I had no control."

"Right," the Witch said. Making fun of the Princess, "Oh, I have all this power, but I don't know how it works. I guess I'll spy on people's most private thoughts without asking."

Brooke didn't back down. "You knew. You let me into your dreams, didn't you?"

The Witch stood up, "Stay out of my head!" she yelled at her and erupted in flames.

The soldiers drew their weapons.

The Witch looked at the fire around her, backed up, and ran off into the night.

"A bit of a temper, that one," the smaller Giant said.

❀ ❀ ❀ ❀ ❀ ❀ ❀

The next night, the Parakeet Prince told his tale. Brooke tried to translate for Lord Hester and his knights, but it got to be too much.

"I'm not trying to get anyone all fired up," Lord Hester said, looking at the Witch, "but may I ask, is the same dream connection you all have responsible for being able to understand Prince Higginbotham?"

"I believe so," Brooke told him. "Somehow it all stems from the Sorcerer's magic."

"Higginbotham?" the taller Giant said. "We know you."

"You're the librarian," the smaller one said.

"Why, yes," Ben said.

When Ben told them the reason for the Sorcerer's jealousy, the Giants got to their feet.

"It'ss your fault," the taller one said. "You sstarted thiss."

"No," Brooke told them.

"You brought his anger down on us," the smaller one blamed Ben.

"Sit down," the Witch yelled at them. "Or I'll sear the skin off your bones."

The Giants quieted down, but they remained standing, breathing heavily.

"This is the Sorcerer's doing, no one else," the Witch went on. "You were there. Tell us, what happened next?"

So, the Giants sat down and began to tell their tale. The taller one started – and it went something like this ...

❀ ❀ ❀ ❀ ❀ ❀ ❀

We're ssissterss, you ssee. Farmerss' wivess, both of uss. Nothing more. 'Ussed to hard work, long dayss.

We took up the King'ss offer of free land outsside a nobleman'ss casstle.

We cleared the land and built our homess. There'ss nothing like working a land that belongss to you. Nothing.

Everything changed the day the Ssorccerer came down out of hiss tower.

You have no idea how a little bit of magic can make the world a better placce.

Everyoness livess got better. You'd finissh your work in half the time, leaving you more time to enjoy yourselvess. We ussed lessss water but grew more deliciouss fruitss and vegetabless.

The Ssorccerer had done ssomething to the pond we drew our water from.

❀ ❀ ❀ ❀ ❀ ❀ ❀

"That's where we were on the day …" the smaller Giant said and then grew quiet, and her head slumped down.

The group watched her as her shoulders rose and fell, faster and faster. One giant tear after another splashed on the ground, forming puddles below.

Her sister Giant continued the story …

❀ ❀ ❀ ❀ ❀ ❀ ❀

We were there, drawing water from the pool when we heard the sscreamss.

The firess came. Our homess … all we had, up in flamess.

We ssaw our hussbandss running acrossss the field, then dissappearing in the ssmoke.

We dove into the pond as the fire came at uss – sstaying under ass long ass we could. When we came up for air, everything wass burnt, everyone wass gone.

We ussed the water to ssave some of the cropss and they … sspread. Grew and died and grew sso fast.

❀ ❀ ❀ ❀ ❀ ❀ ❀

"So did we," the smaller Giant said. And the sisters held each other.

"I'm so sorry ladies," Brooke said.

"Where were you during the fire?" Benjamin asked the Witch, nicely.

"I'd tell you," she said, "… but then I'd have to pluck you."

~ *XX* ~

The Wall

He'd seen it coming. Far off at first: distant echoes of cries, light wisps of smoke.

Each day, louder and closer.

A force to reckon with. Finally. Maybe they could do what he could not.

No matter how many times he had looked over the railing at the ground, hundreds of feet below, he couldn't summon the courage to end it all.

After that horrible day years ago, he found himself here, on the stone floor, as though waking from a dream – the smell of charcoal filling his nostrils. He stared down at the terrible destruction he'd inflicted on the world: homes and barns still burning, clouds of smoke blotting out the sun.

He searched the charred wasteland for survivors. Finding none, he spread the pond of water over the still smoldering fields, hoping to create a living, growing forest, but no sorcery could cure this land. It remained infected with death.

Julianna. What had become of her? When he started the fire, there was a moment where he was sure he put a protective spell on her. Then he saw her consumed in the flames. Again and again, he searched for some sign among the ruins of his library, relieved and hopeful each time he found no evidence of her.

He waited for retribution. Surely, Benjamin's father would come with his soldiers, drag him from his tower, try him for his crimes and put a rope around his neck to end his misery.

They never came.

The evil forest he'd surrounded himself with wouldn't allow it.

But now they were coming. They were coming with the sound of thunder.

❀ ❀ ❀ ❀ ❀ ❀ ❀

For days, they'd been able to see the fortress. Before nightfall, they'd be through the forest. Finally.

"I'll see what I can see," Benjamin told Brooke, the Witch and the Giants.

"Where'ss he going?" the taller Giant whispered to her sister.

"To see if the Sorcerer is home, I guess."

"Of coursse he'ss home," the tall Giant said, still whispering. "Where'ss he going to go?"

"How should I know?" the smaller Giant said. "He's a Sorcerer. He can fly around if he wants to."

"He'ss not a Witch," the tall Giant said.

"Ladies," the Witch yelled out.

"What?" they both said.

"Time to go," the Witch told them.

"Oh, right," the taller one said.

As they'd arranged, the taller Giant cupped Brooke in her enormous hands and moved her to a pocket they'd fashioned in the skins she was wearing.

"There's no door in the wall," Ben reported as he rejoined the group just beyond the tree line.

"He's tricky that way," the smaller Giant said as she set the Witch up on her shoulder.

The taller Giant was on one knee, digging down under the wall.

From inside of her breast pocket, the Princess called out, "Can we go under the wall like Ben's father did?"

"It'ss no good," the taller Giant said, showing the group her dirty arm. "'He's fixxed that, too."

"See, tricky," the smaller Giant said.

Brooke said, "Well, I wouldn't be my mother's daughter if I let a little thing like a wall stop me, now would I?

"Huh?" said the smaller Giant.

"It meanss we're knockin' it down," the giant Giant slurred as she pulled at the closest, largest tree. Together, the Giants managed to rip the tree from its roots and strip the branches, vines, and the beasts that clung to it.

The Witch rolled up her sleeves. She didn't care that she exposed her skeletal arm. "No earth, no water, never grown," she said. "First death, then life, then stone."

The tree fossilized, and they slammed the stone tree into the stone wall.

From his tower, the Sorcerer watched the group ramming the wall. It shook. It cracked with every pounding of the battering ram.

"Too mucchh maggic in the sstoness," the tall Giant said, running short of breath.

"Maybe we need more of our own," Brooke suggested from inside the pocket. "Bring me countess what's-her-name," she demanded.

"What's-her-name? Really?" the Witch said.

The taller Giant gathered up the Witch and put her in her pocket.

"You won't tell us, so ..." Brooke said. She ripped a hole in the Giant's pocket so they could see. "Alright. Once more, with everything," Brooke yelled out.

The lady Giants lifted the tree and retreated a hundred yards (only a few steps for them). Then ran toward the wall.

Just before they slammed into the barricade, the Princess and the Witch yelled, "We are fire," and shot a fireball into the spot where stone crashed against stone – magic into magic – and the earth quaked.

Above them, high in the tower, the Sorcerer was thrown to the floor as his mighty wall tumbled to the ground.

The Witch jumped down as the two Giants covered their heads and bent over. They shielded the Witch, Lord Hester, and his men from the shower of stones with their bodies.

When the dust cleared, they all looked to see the mountain of rock piled high against the Sorcerer's tower.

"Good job," the Parakeet Prince said as he fluttered around the rubble. "You should be able to reach the tower from the top of these stones."

Up high, Beauregard got to his feet and hurried back to the railing. Below, he saw the figures that had been obscured in the dark. "Giants?" he said to himself. "Where did they get giants?"

He took in a deep breath and then sent his booming voice down, "Stay away."

The Giants continued their assent.

The Sorcerer lifted his arms to the sky. Dark clouds moved in blocking the moon. Lightning and thunder followed, then the rains.

"Rain? Really?" the smaller Giant said to the sky. "That's all you got?"

"Don't ever say that," the Witch told her.

"Why?" she asked

Right then a bolt of lightning struck a pile of rubble next to the Giant's hand, scorching it with the heat.

"Oh," she said. "I get it."

Another bolt, and both of the Giants had to scramble to get out of the way.

Just as the Sorcerer was about to raise his arms again to call for another bolt of lightning, the Parakeet Prince shot up from an air stream and attacked, pecking at his face – forcing him back. The bird pecked his eye. Beau screamed. Bolts of lightning shot out from his fingers. Blowing holes in the wall.

Benjamin ducked and dodged.

The Sorcerer finally stopped and placed his hands over his eye, whispered some incantation to heal it. When he pulled his hands away, he saw that there were two female Giants – their massive heads and shoulders appearing above the balcony railing – a Witch, and a Parakeet (along with a Princess peeking through the hole in the Giant's pocket) all staring at him.

~ *XXI* ~

The Tower

"**W**ho are you?"

"Hello, Sorcerer," the Giants said in unison.

The Sorcerer looked more closely at the Giant women. "Do I know you?"

"You murdered our husbandss," the taller one said.

"Both of them," echoed the shorter one.

"You don't have to ssay, both of them," the taller one told her. "I ssaid hussbandss, with an 'ss', that meanss both."

"How am I supposed to know? Your 'sses' last forever," she asked. "Why do you have to correct me all the time?"

"I don't do it all the time."

"That's a correction right there."

"Ladies," the Witch yelled over them.

"Ssorry," they said.

"Do you know me?" the Witch asked the Sorcerer. "Do I

look familiar?" With that, she removed the mask that hid the disfigured half of her face and tore off the black cloak, exposing the burnt flesh and bone that covered half of her body. "No?"

The Sorcerer said, "I don't ..."

"Would you marry me now, Beau?" the Witch said.

The Sorcerer stepped backward, shaking his head. "Julianna?

"Julianna," Ben repeated circling around to get a better look at her.

"Let me out," Brooke yelled from the pocket of the Giant.

Beau started to say, "I thought you were ..." but couldn't finish.

"Dead? You don't know how many times I wished I were. I survived – half of me, anyway. And a few of your books," she told him. "Do you want to see what I learned from them?" Then, to all of them, "Do you all want to see what I learned?"

"Probably not," the small Giant said under her breath.

"Thiss time I agree with you, ssister," the taller one said.

"Let me out," Brooke asked again.

The Giant cupped the Princess in her hands and placed her inside the room.

The Witch/Julianna stretched out her arms. The burnt parts began to grow scales. The scales spread as her body grew, her eyes turned a bright blue color and a tail emerged from behind. Wings sprouted from her back, and her face became lizard-like. The Witch transformed herself into a Dragon right before their eyes, becoming so large she could no longer fit on the balcony. She leaped into the air. "This is what your kind of love can create. Now it's my turn to show you fire!"

"No, Julianna, please," Brooke screamed. "You're better than this."

"I'm really not," she said.

Julianna, the Dragon, sucked in air through her nostrils, and a deep red light glowed in her chest as she was about to burn the Sorcerer with her flaming breath. "I am fire, and you will feel my wrath!"

Brooke pulled the Sorcerer behind her.

"What are you doing?" Julianna yelled.

"I don't know," Brooke said. "Saving you."

"Out of my way, or I'll burn you where you stand," Julianna told her.

"Then that's what you'll have to do," Brooke said.

The Taller Giant moved in front of the Dragon, too.

"What are you doing?" the smaller Giant asked.

"And you'll have to burn me, too," Benjamin said, joining Brooke and the Giant.

"And me, I guess," the smaller Giant lady said, reluctantly positioning herself to block the Dragon.

"What's wrong with you people?" the Dragon asked. "He's evil."

"And you're not," Brooke said.

"He took everything from me," Julianna said.

"Not everything," Brooke said.

"He destroyed me," Julianna said.

"And you've rebuilt yourself," Brooke argued. "Countess,

please."

Julianna, the Dragon, breathed deeper and deeper, growing hotter and hotter, and finally filled the black sky with the fire that was inside of her belly – but it wasn't aimed at the Sorcerer anymore.

The heat of it burned through the storm clouds, exposing the moonlight.

Julianna, the dragon, beat her wings and flew off toward the crescent moon.

"Wow, that wass closse," the taller Giant said. "I thought we were toasst."

"Uh – why did we do that, again?" the shorter one asked.

"Why did you?" the Sorcerer asked.

"I have other plans for you," Brooke told him.

"You have ...? Who are you?" the Sorcerer asked her.

"I'm your redeemer or your executioner," she told him. "So choose your words carefully from here on out."

"Don't test me, girl," the Sorcerer said.

"I'm no girl," she told him. "I'm a Princess, and he is your Lord," she said, pointing to Ben. "I'll test you because I've earned the right to," she told him. "Your master's dead."

"What?" Beau asked?

"I was with him when he passed, and his thoughts were of you. The old man didn't die with disappointment in his eyes," she told him. "He died with hope. Hope of saving you." Brooke took the pouch from her pocket and removed a small jewel on a chain. "He gave me this amulet, for you, and his message to you was, 'I failed to teach you the most important lesson of all: talent without heart is the quickest path to evil.'"

The Sorcerer reached out for it.

"You can't have it yet," she told him, putting it back in the pouch. "You'll have to earn it."

The Sorcerer rose. "Give it to me," he said, through clenched teeth.

"Or what? You'll kill me?" she asked him. "All of us? Even those behind you?" The Princess motioned with her head for the Sorcerer to look behind him.

Lord Hester was there, along with his Knights – all with their weapons drawn.

"An enemy never attacks from only one direction," she told him. "That's why a friend will always say, 'I've got your back.'"

"Clever girl," Ben said.

"Sshhe iss ssmart," the Giant whispered to her sister.

"Really smart," the shorter one whispered back. When her sister glared at her, she shrugged, saying, "What?"

"There you go, repeating me."

"I was agreeing with you. Agreeing isn't repeating."

"Then jusst ssay you agree. Don't ssay the ssame thing as me, ussing different words," the tall Giant argued.

"Ladies," Ben said.

"Right," the Giants said together, nodding.

Brooke asked the Sorcerer, "Do you know what a wizard does with his magic when he passes? I do." Brooke leaned her head back and exhaled golden particles. When she sucked them back in with her next breath, her body grew and changed, larger and larger, becoming a giant version of the old, old Man in his purple robes. She spoke in his voice. "You don't have the magic to defeat me, apprentice. You don't have the skill. You don't have the heart."

"No," the Sorcerer said, bowing his head. "I don't."

Brooke closed her eyes and returned to normal. Everyone in the room was frozen.

"Look at me, Beauregard," Brooke said. "I'll spare you, for now, because you were my mother's friend, once," she told him.

"Your mother?" Beau looked closely at Brooke's face. With a gasp, he realized who she was.

"Yes," the Princess said, "I am my mother's daughter."

"You look like her ..." he said. "Except the eyes, they're a bit more ..."

"Magical?" she asked. "Because I'm the one you cast your spell on – not the Queen."

"Then how could you leave the castle?" he asked.

The Princess smiled, "Your spell was only magic. I had much more powerful weapons: family, friends, love," she said, "And a brain."

"I'll remove it just the same," he told her.

"That's a good place to start," she told him.

Then he waved his arms and wand, saying, "It's winding back, in full reverse – I now release you from your curse."

"It wasn't a curse," she said aloud ...

Ben joined her, along with Hester and his knights, "It was a spell."

"That's it?" she asked, unsure.

"That's it," he said.

Everyone watched, holding their breath, as Princess Brooke took her first tentative step onto the balcony, then another and another. When nothing happened, Brooke spread her arms, laughed out loud and spun around in the open air. "It's wonderful," she said. She ran back and hugged the Sorcerer. "Thank you," she said and kissed his cheek.

"Really, we're kisssssing him, now?" the taller Giant said.

"I thought we were going to eat him. Aren't we going to eat him?" said the small one.

"I know you," the Sorcerer said to the Giants, "you worked one of the farms."

"He can't even remember our names," the shorter one whispered to her sister.

"We're not doing a lot of farming anymore," the taller one told him.

"None, actually," the other said. Her sister glared at her. Realizing she did it again, she said, "I mean, I agree."

"But you can again, if you would wish to," he said to them and raised his wand. "Restitou anterior corpus." (Basically: return to your previous body.)

Nothing happened. The two Giants looked at each other, shrugging their shoulders. Then they both burped and made noises as though they might be sick. The smaller one threw up a large amount of, what looked like, lake water. Then the taller one did the same. They both held onto the railing of the balcony as a huge eruption began to build inside of them. Like a dam bursting, water spewed forth from their bodies, flooding the balcony and tower, drenching everyone.

When the liquid subsided, it exposed two farmer women, back in their human forms, soaked, coughing, holding onto the railing. The knights pulled them back to safety.

It took them a moment of looking at each other – then at their surroundings – to realize what happened. They hugged each other and laughed and cried and couldn't tell which emotion suited the occasion best.

"This is amazing," the shorter Woman said to the Sorcerer. "No wonder she wanted to kiss you."

"Let's not get carried away," the taller Woman said without any kind of slurring at all, and they went back to hugging each other.

With another wave of his wand, the Sorcerer dried off everyone and everything.

"What about my friend here?" Princess Brooke said to the Sorcerer, referring to Ben.

"I'm confused. Who are you exactly?" the Sorcerer asked the Parakeet.

"I'm Prince Benjamin Mordecai Higginbotham," he answered.

"You're alive?" Beauregard asked.

The bird nodded.

"Thank goodness, Your Highness. I thought you'd perished

as well." Beau was almost overcome with emotion. At least he hadn't killed all those he cared for. He leaned against the mirror standing next to him.

"Not everyone died, Sorcerer," the smaller Woman told him.

"I think he's figuring that out," the taller one said to her sister.

The Sorcerer looked back at Ben, confused. "But … you're a bird."

"Yes."

"I thought I turned you into a toad," the Sorcerer said. "Strange." Then he pointed his wand at Prince Benjamin the Parakeet and said, "Go back, go back, from whence you came; in Princely garb and that lengthy name."

Suddenly a rainbow of colors filled the room. Then, just as quickly, disappeared into the night's shadows.

Prince Benjamin was standing there in his human form.

"But I … I kind of liked being a bird," Ben said. "Is it too late to …

Everyone was shocked.

"I'm kidding," the Prince said with a smile. Then turned to face his best friend.

Benjamin was right when he had described himself to the Princess: he didn't seem much like a Prince. He was handsome, in a way: tall, kind eyes, but not particularly regal looking – sort of … ordinary.

That's not at all what the Princess thought as she stared at him. She thought he was … well, kind of perfect.

The Prince bowed to her, "My lady."

"My lord," she said back to him as she curtsied.

"He's much cuter as a human," the taller Woman said.

"Way cuter than he was as a bird," the smaller one added.

"I just said that," the taller Woman told the other.

"Ladies?" Brooke said.

"What?" they both answered.

"You're both right," the Princess said and turned to Prince Benjamin.

And she kissed him. (There've been good kisses throughout history – great ones even – and there'll be more. But few have been so long in the waiting, so instilled with the bonds of friendship and so long deserving. If they hadn't been so madly in love with each other already, this kiss would have done it.)

"Oh my goodness," Brook said, feeling the warmth of the kiss move through her body.

"Oh my goodness," the women repeated, feeling a little warm themselves.

"As for you," Brooke said, turning to face the Sorcerer.

He knelt before her. "Your Highness," he said. "If there's anything I can do–"

"You can be quiet for one thing," she told him.

Everyone was shocked at how Brooke spoke to him – no one more than Beau himself.

"Does that anger you, Sorcerer?" she asked him. "We've seen what your temper can do."

"No, Your Highness," he said, quietly.

"Good. Because if you're truly repentant, then I may have a path of redemption for you," she said.

"I would give anything to right the wrongs I've committed," he said.

"I'll hold you to it," she told him. "You'll walk every inch of land that's grown diseased by your hateful magic, reverse its spell, and plant anew. It may take the rest of your life. Are you willing to do this?"

"I am," he said, still on his knees.

"Then rise, Sorcerer."

Beau stood up. The Princess took his hand in hers. She held out her other hand to her friend. "Ben?"

Prince Benjamin took Brooke's hand. "I have something to show you," she said as she walked them toward the balcony railing. "You'll have plenty of help, Beauregard," she said.

The men looked down. An entire army, with torches blazing, spread out below among the ruins of the Sorcerer's wall.

Ben's hand went to cover his mouth. "My eyes aren't as good as they were a few minutes ago, but is that …?"

"Yes, my friend. Your father has come to greet you."

Below them, the King, Ben's father, stood high upon the stones of the broken wall and waved to his son.

Ben was overwhelmed. He couldn't help himself. He grabbed Brooke in his arms and kissed her, then held her tight. "Thank you, thank you," he said in her ear.

"What are friends for?" she said

He released her so he could look into her beautiful face. His smile could have lit up the sky.

"Finally," she said. "I get to see you smile."

~ *XXII* ~

New Growth

tep by step, one patch of forest after another the Sorcerer, the sisters, soldiers from both kingdoms, a Prince, a Princess, and sometimes even a King set to work reclaiming the land.

The first thing Beauregard did was to make the castle tower and remnants of the great wall disappear.

No more walls.

The next challenge was to clear the road to the east, leading to Benjamin's family's castle.

Beau unleashed an incantation that stopped the endless growth of the forest. The beasts, vegetation, and insects were another story. They had to be dealt with one at a time.

Brooke wouldn't allow the Sorcerer to use fire. She wanted Beau to face his demons and do the work to reclaim the land. Every tree had to be felled; roots had to be pulled from the ground.

❀ ❀ ❀ ❀ ❀ ❀ ❀

On this day, the Sorcerer was ahead of everyone (he was always in the lead) when he came upon a grove of trees set close together, with an open space at the center.

He put his hand on the bark of one of them. It felt warm to the touch. He hurried forward, placing a hand on each trunk: heat emanated from every one.

It was when he reached the edge of the grove that he heard it. Right away, he realized the stupidity of racing too far ahead of everyone. It was the low, slurping growl of beasts. He turned slowly to face a pack of two-headed dogs; lips curled, nostrils flared, black saliva dripping from rows of sharp, hungry teeth – the animals were three times the size of any wolves he'd ever seen with needles for fur.

Beau stepped gingerly back into the grove. The lead animal put one paw forward, but when it tried going forward with another, it stopped. The Sorcerer took a few more steps back. The pack spread out around the edge of the grove but didn't cross the line of trees; they couldn't, or wouldn't.

"Restitou anterior corpus," Beauregard said to each of the beasts, aiming his wand. Within minutes, a group of friendly mutts was jumping and barking and playing with each other. No longer afraid of the grove, some rushed to the Sorcerer, licking his hand and begging for affection.

Lord Hester, Ben, and the King arrived at the entrance of the grove, swords drawn, ready for action. Relieved to find Beau safe, they were immediately affected by the trees. They, too, felt a need to touch the trunks.

Brooke entered shortly after, leading a squad of armed soldiers, the sisters following. The Princess had an arrow at the ready, relaxing it when she found all was well. "What is this place?" she asked Beau.

"I don't know," he answered.

"It's the grove I told you about," Ben said.

"I know what it is," the King said. "I know who it is." He was standing between two beautiful white sycamore trees, a hand on each. "Trees like this never grow in a dense forest; they need open air – but look how tall and strong they've grown," he said with tears welling up in his eyes.

Benjamin understood and went to his father. He, too, placed one hand on each tree. After a time, the two men hugged each other.

Brooke motioned for everyone to leave the King and Prince alone. The rest gathered in the open space in the center of the grove.

"They must have made camp here," Lord Hester said, figuring out the landscape. "Over a hundred men. This would have been the fire, where we're standing. The King's sons, together, there," pointing to the two trees where Ben and his father now sat, talking. "It probably happened while they slept."

"Can you bring them back?" Brooke asked Beauregard.

"I'll do everything in my power."

He did. The Sorcerer tried every spell, every potion, herb or incantation he could think of – day and night, without sleep.

On his knees, tortured, and beyond weary, Beauregard felt a strong hand on his shoulder.

"That's enough," the King told him. "Let them rest now."

Father and son marked the two trees with the royal crest and left the grove just as it was. No one was allowed to touch it. They would clear the land around it, keeping an eye out for surrounding trees that had once been sentries and scouts for the company – so as not to uproot them.

"I've had enough," the King told Ben afterward. "When you're finished here, I hope you'll come home. Your mother and brothers miss you terribly."

"I will, father," Ben said, shaking the King's hand.

Both men looked over at Brooke who was helping the Sorcerer to his feet. She saw them both looking and smiled.

"She'll have something to say about where we go next," Ben said.

"I'm sure she will," the King said, smiling. Then he grabbed his son and held him close. "You're not allowed to die anymore – not while I'm alive. You got that?" he told his favorite son.

"Yes, sir," Ben said.

When the King finally let his boy go, he turned quickly and walked away, keeping his head high.

❀ ❀ ❀ ❀ ❀ ❀ ❀

As they reclaimed more and more of the forest from the evil that had overtaken it, the monsters had fewer places to hide.

Beau only saw a flash of movement out of the corner of his eye, in the tangled underbrush: a thick tube of slithering scales and two large, reptilian eyes. The first bite nearly took his foot clean off. The next chomp of its hinge-less jaws shattered his kneecap.

Just as the serpent spread its mouth open, wide enough to snap him in two, Beau's wand pierced its marble-like eye. At the same time, he felt two arms dragging him backward, and he watched as Ben and Lord Hester sliced into the tough hide of the snake with their blades.

Hester's swordsmanship was more like a dancer's movements: effortlessly sidestepping the croc-serpent's coiling body he cut off leg after leg, both sets of wings springing from its back, and then he smoothly chopped off the rattling tail bit by bit.

Brooke called for a physician and pushed Beau to the ground. "Sit still," she told him.

The Princess ripped the sleeve from her blouse and tied it around the Sorcerer's leg. Then she ripped off the other sleeve.

"I don't understand," he told her, half-scared, half-angry, "I welcome death. Why don't I accept it when it's offered to me?"

"I can't say why you do what you do," she answered. "Stay alive if you can …" The Princess concentrated on binding the Sorcerer's ankle, having already secured the knee – tying it off with a forceful pull of the knot. "Do some good."

"That was disgusting," Ben said.

The two of them looked up to see the Prince covered in some kind of green blood and goo.

"So much for the librarian I fell for," Brooke said.

Brooke spotted the physician. "Good, a real doctor." She got up but turned back to Beau before she left. "Bad news, you're probably going to live."

❀ ❀ ❀ ❀ ❀ ❀ ❀

Now and then Ben would catch the Princess searching the skies – especially at night after the day's work was done. He didn't have to ask her why. Sometimes she'd sit in his lap and lay her head on his shoulder, and they'd stare at the stars together.

"I worry about her."

"I know, Love," he'd say.

"She doesn't think she needs us, but she does."

Then Ben did what good friends do when you're puzzled and sad: he just stuck with Brooke. "She'll figure it out," he said.

"'You think so?" the Princess asked; really asked.

"I'm sure of it," Ben told her. "She'll find you when she needs you."

The Princess would squeeze his hand tighter. She would always hold his hand.

❀ ❀ ❀ ❀ ❀ ❀ ❀

It was two years into the revival of the forest. Most of the forest had been cleared, but there was still one area left untouched.

The two Sisters couldn't bring themselves to return to the farms where they lost their husbands.

It'd been cleared of insects and animals, but the wood remained a dark stain while all around it the sun began to shine.

Benjamin and his father decided to locate relatives of anyone who'd perished in the fires and bequeath them plots of land, seed, cattle, and enough silver to get them started. That way, those who'd lost the most to this land were able to benefit from it.

Craftsmen, tradesmen, and the like soon joined the settlers. Where there was once a camp, the makings of a town sprang up: dry goods store, blacksmith's, barracks for the soldiers.

At the center was an enormous inn with a hundred rooms that Brooke's father had donated, so the relatives could have food and lodging until their homes and farms were ready (and to make sure his daughter had a decent place to stay). Brooke sent for the innkeeper to run the place.

They gathered in the dining hall as they usually did at the start of each day. Everyone was strong and tanned from working outdoors – even the Sorcerer, whose skin had long since lost its green tint.

Brooke dabbed her mouth with a napkin, placed it on the table and turned her attention to the two Sisters arguing with each other at the end of the table. Ben did the same. Then Lord Hester. Then Beau.

When the Sisters realized everyone was looking at them, they grew silent.

"We think it's time you worked some land of your own," said Brooke.

"As many acres as you want," Ben added. "We'll have a home of your choosing built, find servants to help you, and supply you with all the livestock and seed you require."

"Whatever you need," said Beau.

The two women looked at each other, squinting. Then back at them.

"Is there money involved?" asked the taller Sister.

"How would we pay the servants?" the smaller one said.

"The King has asked me to give you a thousand pieces of silver, for your service," Ben told them.

"A thousand?" the smaller one asked.

"More if you need it," he said.

"More, then," the other said. "I'm thinking, yes, more."

"Definitely, more," her sister added.

"Since he offered."

"Fine," Beau said with a little crooked smile. (He'd been smiling more and more recently.) "Then it's settled."

"We have a patch of land I think would be just right for you," Brooke told them.

The Sisters agreed to look at it. "Just look, that's all – no promises," the taller Sister said, eyeing Beau. A smiling Beau made her suspicious.

The smaller Sister, not so much. She kept whispering to her Sister in a higher and higher pitch, "We're going to be rich. We're going to be rich. We're going to be rich."

Beau, limping, led them past newly grown pastures and farmlands, tended by the new owners.

"This is exciting," the smaller Sister said to the other. She was eating an apple one of the farmers had given them as they passed through his orchard.

"We'll see," the taller one said, not convinced, and took a bite of hers. "You know, this work – this whole foresting thing – could have gone a lot faster if we were still giants," she told Beau.

"Maybe you could turn us back, and we could make quick work of the rest of it," the shorter one added.

"That's kind of what I said," the taller one said to her friend.

"Yes, but not exactly," said the shorter one.

"Well, it's close enough."

"Ladies!" Beau said.

"What?" they asked together.

It was then that they realized where they were; back at their old farm – one of few remaining traces of the day that marked the end of their happiness.

"Why would you bring us here?" the smaller Sister asked.

"Your heart is still just as black as ever," said the taller one.

"No," he told them simply.

They looked, and Beauregard was standing between two of the largest, most beautiful oak trees they had ever seen; the trunks were four times the thickness of a man, arms stretching out in every direction, ultimately reaching toward the heavens with a greenery of life that could not be denied.

The half-eaten apple of one Sister fell to the ground, another core followed. As though in a trance they each walked up to a different tree as if they'd been drawn to it, gently stretched their arms around the trunk and placed their cheeks upon the bark.

Beau, Ben, Brooke, and Lord Hester watched as the trees softly bent their branches around the women, hugging them in return.

"It's not a dead forest anymore," Brooke said.

Each of them silently agreed.

~ *XXIII* ~

The Road Home

here was no more evil forest. The village was thriving.

The two Sisters invited them all to their newly built mansion for an extravagant dinner. They argued as much as they always had.

The Prince and Princess were growing restless, anxious to start their lives together.

Brooke visited Lord Hester at the barracks to tell him to prepare the company for travel.

"Yes ... of course, Your Highness," he said.

Brooke searched his face. "What are you not telling me?"

"If I may," he asked.

"Of course you may. Please do," she said.

"Several of the men have expressed an interest in staying behind."

She smiled. "Really?" she asked.

"Yes, my lady. There must be something about fighting to

reclaim a patch of land that makes you feel, well, responsible for it," Hester said.

"I see," she said. "Are you one of these men?"

"Your Highness, I would never shirk my responsibilities."

"I think you've more than proved that," she said. "That wasn't actually my question, though."

"Yes, Your Highness, I wish to stay on," he admitted.

"I think that's a lovely idea," she told him. "I'll speak to the Prince, and we'll arrange for you all to receive the same compensation as the others. Wait. It's not the whole company is it?"

"A handful, Your Highness," he told her.

The Princess took a moment to look at this man who'd been her teacher, her protector, and her friend. She smiled at him, went up on her tippy-toes, and whispered in his ear, "I'll miss you." Then kissed his cheek.

"Keep your eye on Beau," she said over her shoulder as she left.

❀ ❀ ❀ ❀ ❀ ❀ ❀

The morning they were scheduled to leave, Brooke walked toward the head of the troop with her stallion keeping pace behind her. Ben was a step or so behind.

Beau approached the Princess and handed her a bag of seeds. "These are for your mother ... and father. Please tell them that with these they can start a new orchard."

Brooke looked at the bag for a long time and then said, "Umm, no," and handed him back the bag. "Do it yourself."

The Sorcerer looked at the bag, shaking his head. "I don't

know that I could ever face them," he said to himself as much as to Brooke.

"Don't you think you should find out?" she asked

Beau didn't know what to say. He stared at the bag.

Brooke patted her horse's neck, and he knelt so she could easily mount. She grabbed hold of his mane and swung up on the stallion's back.

"Your Highness," Beau said, "may I have the gift from my master? The amulet?"

"No," she said.

Beau looked around. "Why not? It's mine."

"Not until I give it to you, it isn't," she told him.

"You keep pushing me," he said.

"That's right, Sorcerer," she told him, leaning closer to him. "Because when you get pushed, you break, and when you break, people get hurt."

He nodded. Not happy about it, but knowing it was true.

"Find a way to get rid of your powers," she told him. "Then we'll talk."

She looked over to Ben. "Why am I the one who's supposed to have all the answers? I'm the youngest person here."

"Because you're a Queen," he told her.

"I'm only a Princess."

"Only a Princess?" he said, looking at her sideways.

"Alright, that's a lot," she admitted, smiling.

"I'm pretty sure you'll be a queen someday," he said.

"What? Why?" she asked him.

He just smiled and rode past her.

Brooke spurred her horse forward.

As the couple approached the crowd of people gathered to say their goodbyes, Brooke asked Ben, "Remember back at the inn? Julianna was wrong – she predicted I wouldn't make it to the end of the journey."

"Yes, so ...?" Ben said, confused. "Oh. Wait. You think this is the end of our journey?"

"What?"

"Wave," Ben said.

"What?"

"Wave. Your hand," Ben said, waving his hand. They were in the middle of the crowd of well-wishers now.

The Princess and the Prince waved goodbye to the Sisters in their fancy carriage yelling, "WooHoo," to Lord Hester and the remaining soldiers saluting them, and to the many townspeople.

Further down the road, after their arms grew tired, Brooke took in a peaceful breath and let it out. "Good. Okay," she said and got in tune with the movement of her great stallion.

After a few minutes, she realized she'd been staring down at the hard gravel road and naturally fell into her meditation. "Oh, my goodness," she said to herself, looking up and all around, "I've only been able to see the roads I traveled – never the world around it." She laughed out loud at the thought.

"You're going to love it," Ben said. "It's beautiful. And mostly good."

Looking over to her Prince, smiling back at her: "Where to, my Prince?" she said, spreading her arms out wide, "We have the whole, wide world to choose from."

"Let's see it all. First my place, then yours, then who knows?" he said. "You've never even seen the ocean, have you?"

"Ahh, that's right. There are oceans to cross," she said with her eyes open wide.

"I didn't ... I didn't mention crossing," he said.

Princess Brooke laughed out loud again.

"Perhaps we'll just keep going until we've had our fill," Ben said.

"What would make you think I could ever get my fill?" she asked.

"Good point," he said and smiled.

And they rode off together ... with Princess Brooke on a horse named Hope.

RINCESS

ROOKE

If I could only explain the effect Brooke Hester has had on my life. As a writer, I've been blessed with the skills to do it, yet I keep falling short.

Brooke and her mother showed up at the launch party for my book, *The Princess Fables*, in Corpus Christi, Texas in spring, 2014. They'd traveled an hour to see me, even though Brooke had been very ill. She had a present for me: a lovely Crayola illustration titled, Mermaid Cowgirl Princess.

I asked Brooke if she'd like to help with my next book, *The Royal Fables: Stories From the Princes & Princesses of the Texas Children's Hospital.* It would be a collection of short stories I'd write based on titles and illustrations the patients at TCH made up. All of the proceeds would benefit pediatric brain cancer research at the hospital. Brooke had been treated there, so she was a perfect choice.

When *The Royal Fables* was published, I headed to the Ronald McDonald House in Houston to visit her. Two of her illustrations were in the book along with the story I wrote based on her title: *The Princess Who Was Too Demanding* (she was not at all, by the way). She was dressed in a pink cowgirl outfit with a pink cowboy hat, wearing a surgical mask.

The last time I saw this little Princess was in a hospital in New York City. She was very weak. When she was finally able to sit up, I told her I'd brought some of my new stories to read to her, and she said, "Really? I thought you were here so I could give you another idea for a story." Her idea was *The Princess & The Parakeet*.

I started writing this book shortly after that visit and hoped to finish it in time for Brooke to read it, but that wasn't meant to be. Brooke Hester was eight years old when she died. Maybe her family can find some comfort in this tribute to their extraordinary little girl.

Different people grieve in different ways. My way was to try to create something Brooke would have enjoyed. I hope you do, too.

In her spirit, every copy of *The Princess & The Parakeet* sold will include a donation to her charity: Brooke's Blossoming Hope - find out more at www.BrookesBlossoms.org.

PAGE OF GRATITUDE

For your Generosity of Spirit,
In Admiration of your Kindness,
My humble Thanks
- Marc Clark

Dominic Randolf & Riverdale Country School

Nancy Goodman

Tammy Watts

Anonymous

Bryan & Josie Clark

Toby, Melissa, & Princess Anna Coston,

Roseanne Crandall

Al Dodds

Cynthia Hardeman

Taffy & Scot Harlan

Dr. Meyers & Judy Herdon

Scott Humpal

Brooke Karzen

Michelle Moffitt

Scott & Kathy Preston

Ben Suzi, Kalen, & Jace Tuety

Marc Clark

with Brooke Hester

Marc Clark was born into an acting family and started off writing stage plays - his first one was produced in New York City. Then he wrote some screenplays, wrote and produced a couple thousand commercials and the show 30x30 Kid Flicks for HBO Family.

Now he writes fairytales, legends, and myths and visits schools and hospitals a lot (has personally read to over 15,000 kids and young adults in the last few years).

❀ ❀ ❀ ❀ ❀ ❀ ❀

THE PRINCESS & THE PARAKEET, won Cover Design Of the Year at the Southern California Book Festival. That was cool.

THE PRINCESS & THE PARAKEET, won Best Children's Book at the London Book Festival. That was *really* cool.

Check out the website, www.TheFablesKingdom.com and the online store, www.TheFablesKingdom.com/store/

Online Store: www.TheFablesKingdom.com/store
more fun stuff at - www.TheFablesKingdom.com

Find us on **f**
@AuthorMarcClark

AuthorMarcClark @ | *Instagram*

"Read. Read anything. Read the things they say are good f you, and the things they cl are junk. You'll find what need to find. Just read

– Neil Gaiman

Marc Clark
@AuthorMarcClark

You can do anything if you believe in yourself. #FablesKingdom

15 Dec 2018

Made in the USA
Middletown, DE
12 March 2022

62407663R00156